THE CASIQUE FAMILY

Us Before Anything

BRII TAYLOR

An Urban Love Story

CONTENTS

Untitled   v
A Word from The Author   vii

Chapter 1   1
Chapter 2   11
Chapter 3   23
Chapter 4   43
Chapter 5   53
Chapter 6   65
Chapter 7   75
Chapter 8   85
Chapter 9   105
Chapter 10   119
Chapter 11   127
Chapter 12   135
Chapter 13   145
Chapter 14   155
Chapter 15   163
Chapter 16   167
Chapter 17   177
Chapter 18   183
Chapter 19   197

Facebook: Brii Taylor
Facebook Like Page: Ms. Brii
Instagram: authoressbriitaylor
Twitter: taylor_brii
Email: authoressbrii@yahoo.com
Website: www.justbriitaylor.com
Join my reader's group to keep up with new/upcoming releases,
get sneak peeks, giveaways and more!

A WORD FROM THE AUTHOR

Thank you so much for supporting me. I truly appreciate it. I'm just a girl from Portland with a passion for writing. Never did I ever see myself being a published author. Every day, I thank God because it was all him.

As you read this book, I pray you feel and enjoy the characters. This book came out of me like water running from a faucet. It means so much to me. So, thank you for taking yet another ride with me.

As always, I ask that you leave a review with thoughts. Also, if you do leave a review, please don't give the book away.

Happy reading!

CHAPTER 1
ISRAEL "RELL" CASIQUE

"**O**kay, so remind me of the reason we're picking her up again?" Keyona, my fiancée of two and a half years, asked with her hand out and head cocked to the side.

I had to suppress my laughter because her facial expression reminded me of the chick in the memes going around on social media. Y'all know the girl with the long face, little ponytail, and no edges.

"I agreed to be the designee. You knew that though, bae," I said in the sweetest, most calm tone. If I had the slightest twinge of attitude in my voice, she'd cop one back.

Don't get me wrong. I could handle it. Tonight, though, I just wanted to chill. I wanted to have a perfectly civil night with my woman and fam.

It was my pops birthday. He was turning fifty. We wanted to do it big for him since the nigga was now half of one hundred. We had the whole *Club 8*, located in downtown Chicago, rented out just for him. He didn't want a big shindig, but we weren't trying to hear that. This was our pops big day. We had to do it big for him.

"Mmnt!" Keyona smacked her teeth and rolled her eyes. *Here we go*, I palmed my face. I hated when she made a big deal out of nothing. That's exactly what she was about to do with this situation.

Dear Lord, give me strength, I prayed to God for myself.

"I'm just saying. Why she had to ride with us? Isi and Lah car was full?" She was referring to my older and younger brothers, Isiah and Islah.

"No. I'm the designee for *all* of us," I revealed. Closing my eyes, I did a countdown because she was about to turn up on my ass. I hadn't told her I was the designee for all of us.

Us consisted of my older brother, Isi and sister-in-law, Iyanna. Then, there was Lah and whoever he was bringing as a date — *if he had one*. Finally, Paris, my bestest friend in the world, who went by Rizz, and my baby sis, Liz. Her name was Eliza. However, we called her Liz for short. I was scooping Rizz first, then making my way toward Isi's and Lah's. Liz was at Isi's crib, so that was a three for one deal.

Five...four...three...two...one...

"Oh, hellll no! Nope! You didn't talk this over with me first, Rell!" She snapped her neck my way so hard I heard it crack. Shit, I was surprised her head didn't fall off.

"The fuck you mean, I didn't *discuss it with you*?! You ain't my fucking mother, Keyona! Last I checked, I'm a grown ass man! I don't need permission to let my people ride in the car."

See, this was what I was trying to avoid. Now, my

mood was all fucked up. Keyona sure knew how to blow a fucking high. Nonetheless, I loved the hell out this girl.

From the corner of my eye, I could see her bottom lip quivering and eyes watering up. To have so much mouth Keyona was sensitive as fuck. While she could be a complete bitch, she had this soft/sensitive side to her. That's what made me fall in love with her. She was a rude chick. She reminded of an ant at times—hard on the outside, and soft on the inside.

I could only stand her rude side for so long. After a while, I'd end up praying I wouldn't slap her silly ass. My mama taught me to keep my hands to myself when it came to females. Only God himself could stop me from putting hands on Keyona's smart-mouthed ass. I guess it's true what they say. The same way they caught you was going to be how they lost you.

I didn't want to leave Keyona. Like I said, I loved this woman. At one point, I saw her being my wife and having my kids. That is, if she lost the bitchy attitude.

"Baby, you know I love you and I wasn't trying to come for you. All I'm saying is, I shouldn't have to ask your permission to kick it with my fam or go clubbing and be the designee. Like, fuck man. It's my pops birthday and shit. You have to grow up and get along with my family at some point, ma."

"How do you—" she started to yell but I cut her off, holding my finger in her face. She knew I didn't play that shit. Keyona had this habit of yelling to get her point across. I told her, from the first time she tried to raise her voice at me that I wasn't going to tolerate it.

"How do you expect me to get along when they're the ones that hate me? I've done nothing to them!"

"Lower your voice."

"I've done nothing to them," she repeated the last part of her statement. This time, her voice was a little softer and whiny.

I gave her a *nigga please* look. "Don't play victim, ma. You know why they don't fuck with you."

"Ugh, whatever!" She threw her hands up in defeat. "I don't come around as often as they'd like. So, what? Why does that matter, Rell? I'm with you, not them!"

"You know how I am about my family. You could at least try and get along with them. If you're going to be my wife, you need to be cordial enough to get along with them. I'm not saying bake a pie or some shit. Just quit being such a bitch."

"Excuse me, Israel?" She looked me upside the head like I smelled bad or something.

I wasn't taking shit back. I meant what I said. Knowing I wasn't one to apologize for speaking my mind, she turned in her seat to look out the window. I knew she was about to start crying or whatever. Shit, she'd be alright. It wasn't like I was flat out calling her a bitch. She was just acting like one.

Keyona knew how I felt about my fam. They were everything to me. Growing up in a well-established, two parent home with two brothers and a sister, we were solid. Sure, we fought like any other family. At the end of the day, it was *us before anything*.

When I got with Keyona, they were cool at first. That is, until they officially met Keyona. At first, I wasn't bringing her around. I wasn't scared or nothing. We weren't as serious in the beginning. I didn't like bringing females around the fam unless I was serious about them. Too much emotion got involved. My sisters started to get close with her and mama wanted to tell me she wasn't the *one* or whatever.

Once we made shit official, I took her to meet them. Again, they were cool. She was cool. Three months down the line, and she started to feel some type of way. She was complaining about being around my people all the time. She said we spent too much time together and ain't no family *that happy* with each other.

Personally, I didn't see what she meant. I mean, I worked with my dad and brothers. Of course, I'm going to see them all the time. My mom and grandma liked to have family dinner at least two Sundays out the month. Our birthdays were a little close, maybe. Other than that, we were doing our own thing. I didn't get it.

It got so bad that I started throwing caution to the wind when it came to them. This was all to keep her happy and stress-free. I'd make up little excuses why I couldn't attend this function and that function.

All because Keyona always wanted me to herself. I won't put the blame on her, though. I was feeling her so much that I didn't mind giving her all my time. When I loved, I loved hard. I tried to give one hundred percent and expected the shit in return.

Everything was going smooth between us, until one day my family came to me. I showed up at work and was told there was a meeting in the boardroom. They so dramatic, they had the shit set up like an AA meeting or something. There was also a banner that read: *Rell's Intervention*.

Everybody took turns going up to the podium. They all poured out how they felt. At the end of the 'intervention', I felt like shit. I assumed they were cool. I know I missed a few dinners, but that was it.

After that day, I made a change. I was coming around a lot more and made it a point to never miss another family dinner. I wanted my family to feel just as included as Keyona did. Now, everybody was happy. Well...except Keyona.

She hated how close I was with my family. I felt like most of her irritation came from her not being close with hers. I tried to help her reach out to them. I suggested different ways to break the ice that was blocking their bond. There was counseling, phone calls, or my families favorite, popping up and showing your face from time to time.

She wouldn't go for any of it. There was only so much you could do to help someone. Fiancée or not, I wasn't about to force her to do what she didn't want to.

I advised her to get used to my family being around or bounce. She'd been sticking around for this long and hadn't learned to accept it. Yet, she still stayed with me. Honestly, I was getting tired of this shit. I wished she would just grow the fuck up.

I put up with her bullshit because I loved her ass. Plus, she ain't have nobody. From what she told me, her mom or pops didn't really care what she did growing up.

While mine were strict and made sure me, my brothers and sister had the best education, hers didn't even care if she graduated or not.

I guess you could say I felt bad, in a way. I know that's a fucked-up reason to stay with somebody, but aye, it is what it is. I'd been with her this long and put up with it.

"Baby, I love you. I just want to have a great night for

my pops. We can fight about this shit later, okay?" I promised her, caressing her soft brown, manicured hand. She snatched it away and sucked her teeth.

"Yeah, whatever Rell. It doesn't matter how I feel anyway because you're always going to put them before me. Just once, I want it to be us only. Not your brothers, sister, parents, or..." She stopped mid-sentence, looking ahead with a scowl etched on her forehead. "*Her.*"

Looking ahead, I saw what she saw, and a smile emerged on my face. My best friend looked gorgeous as fuck! She was rocking all-white and gold, just like Keyona and I. We were all going to be rocking white and gold. It was the theme for Pops' party.

Sauntering over, Rizz was wearing an all-white dress that stopped a little past her knees. It was long-sleeved and had a deep dip in the front, showing off some of her cleavage. Anybody else who put this dress on, it would've been too much.

Rizz made it look good. Like, it wasn't screaming, 'I'm a ratchet hoe', yet it also wasn't screaming 'I'm a stuck-up hoe'. To top it off, she added a pair of black open-toed heels, some gold diamond earrings, and a necklace.

"Yassss, that's my bestfran, that's my bestfran! You betta!" I poked my head out the window with a big grin on my face. She stopped in the middle of her driveway to strike a pose. "Yaaas guh, you better werk it, hunty!"

Rizz doubled over, laughing her ass off. "Oh lord, you so irri. I swear."

Getting out of the car, I gave her a big hug. It was always like this whenever we saw each other. We played all-day. That was just us. Keyona hated it, but what didn't she hate? Nonetheless, I loved her and didn't let her attitude get to me.

"You love me though, ma," I kissed her cheek.

"Yeah, yeah, yeah…" She waved me off. Taking a step back, she examined what I had on. This was something we'd done to each other for years. "Check you out, okay, okay. Looking dapper, my guy."

"Well thank you, thank you." I took a bow.

I was rocking an all-white Versace linen suit. I had on some white and gold Versace sneakers and sunglasses to match. To finish the fit, I added gold jewelry. It was just a small gold chain and a gold Rolex.

"Are y'all done or…" Keyona did that girl from the meme face again.

Rizz broke out laughing. Again, I had to suppress my laughter. If I had laughed with Rizz, Keyona would've felt singled out. That was one of the main reasons she never came around my family.

"Oh, Relly!" Rizz exclaimed from the back like she'd forgot something. Looking at the clock, we had a little time before the festivities started. If I had to turn back for her, I would.

"What's up?"

"You remember my cousin, Kori?"

Looking at her through the rearview mirror, I made eye contact. "You mean the short, thick, fine one?"

"Rell!" Keyona swatted my bicep. I looked at her and smirked.

"I'm just playing baby, damn."

"Mhm, if you say so! Don't get fucked up in front of your little friend." She rolled her neck and eyes in opposite directions. I always found that creepy, but cool. It was like some exorcist shit.

Giving her a death stare, I silently dared her to do something. Keyona knew damn well she didn't speak to me like that. Not in front of company, not ever. She was showing her ass because Rizz was in the car. She didn't want me to show mine back. I'd really have her insecure ass crying.

"Anyway," Rizz scoffed in a bored tone. I wasn't looking her way, but knew she was rolling her eyes. She couldn't stand Keyona, and the feeling was mutual.

Along with neglecting my family, I had neglected my best friend as well. Once I got back in good graces with the fam, I tried to do the same with Rizz. Rizz wasn't as forgiving as my brothers, sister and parents. I had to beg her uglass and really put in work to get back into her good graces.

"I invited her to Pops' party. Is that cool?"

Pulling up to a stop sign, I glanced in the rearview mirror. "You're seriously asking that question?"

"It's not my party. I had to come correct or not at all." She shrugged her shoulders.

"Yet you invited her to the party. What if I said no and she showed up at the door?" I challenged with a smirk.

"Boy, please! I knew you were going to say yes." She laughed. "So, can she?"

"No," I said in an even tone. I was just playing, but wanted to see what her response would be.

"Relly!" she whined.

"*Rizzy!*" I mimicked her tone.

"Whatever. She can come." Rizz made the decision. She was laughing like it was that funny.

"Then what fuck you ask me for?" I sucked my teeth, pretending to be upset.

"To waste your time, nigga!" She was back to laughing.

"Fucker," I laughed, mimicking Baby Joker from *Next Friday*.

For the rest of the car ride, me and Rizz went back and forth while Keyona stayed quiet. Every so often, I'd look her way and catch her making an annoyed face or rolling her eyes as she texted whomever on her phone. I was determined not to let her get to me tonight. Like I said, it was my pops night. She either got with the program or bounced. Simple as that.

CHAPTER 2
KORI BRYANT

"I'm telling you right now. My cousin invited me to this party. My name should be on the list. It's Kori B—"

"Bryant. I heard you the first time. Yeah right, and my name is Shaquille O'Neal. What do you know?" the bouncer at the door cut me off as I was trying to explain who I was and why I'd shown up at *Club 8*.

"I'm serious. My cousin invited me to this party. Her name is Paris. *They call her Rizz?*" I was trying to get him to believe me. It was cold as fuck outside, and I was in a two-piece shirt and skirt set. To top it off, I'm anemic. His bald-headed fat ass was playing with my life!

"Right. If you say so, sweetheart. Get back so I can let the next set of people in."

"Ugghh!" I stomped off to the side. Since I didn't drive my car, I had to suffer the cold Chicago breeze. I took an Uber because I planned to get white girl wasted tonight. I'd recently finished my last final and was about to graduate at the end of May. This turn up couldn't have come any sooner.

Paris told me it was for her 'Pops' fiftieth birthday. Still, none of that mattered. All I heard was free drinks and a good time. Finding her name in my phone, I set up the call to FaceTime her. It rang three times before she finally picked up.

"Heeyyy, baby cousiiiin! Where you at?!" She sounded like she'd been having the best time of her life. I could see people behind her, and they looked happy as well. Shit, I wanted to be just as great. However, Steve Wilkos' fat ass twin wouldn't let me in the door.

"Hey, beautiful! Can you or somebody please come down and get me? *Apparently*, my name isn't on the list, and this bouncer dude won't let me come inside." I didn't, for a second, hide the irritation in my voice.

"Oh, what?! See, Don big ass doing too much. Hold on, baby. Let me find someone. If I go down the stairs, I might fall." She giggled. Her face was all in the camera. I had to laugh too. Paris was twisted. Shit, I was trying to be on her level, fa'real. I kept my eyes on the screen until I heard her yelling for someone. "Lah-Lah! Comere!"

It took a minute, but the person came. I couldn't see his face, just heard his voice. "What's up, sis?"

"Can you go down and get my cousin? Don being an asshole and won't let her in." Paris rolled her eyes for emphasis.

"Yeah, I got you. Drunk ass." I saw his hand come across the screen as he reached for her head and mushed her.

"Whatever, punk!" She giggled and then turned her attention back to the screen. "Okay, boo. Lah gon let you in. Just hold on."

"Okay, cuzzy!" I smiled before hanging up.

Confidently, I walked back to the front of the line. There was something about knowing I was covered that boosted my confidence. Boldly, I stood in line with my head held high, not speaking a word. Ol' fat ass was too busy running his mouth to notice I was standing there like I never left.

"Oh, you're back again." I guess he finally noticed me. "You seriously trying to make it huh, lady?"

Silence.

I wasn't speaking a peep to this lousy bastard. If I said anything, I'd have him somewhere feeling sorry for himself. My mother always told me *'if you don't have anything nice to say, don't say it at all'*. Tonight, I was abiding by that rule.

"Oh, so you're just going to stand there on your phone like you're invincible?" He laughed. The guy standing next to him chortled a little but didn't say anything verbally. "Let me guess. Your name is *magically* on the list somehow? Who's dick you about to su—"

"Shut yo ass up, Donald."

Just when he was about to say *suck*, the same voice I'd heard on Paris' phone called out to him. Fat ass looked in the man's direction and instantly grew red in the face.

Looking up from my phone, my eyes landed in the light brown pools that belonged to the voice. He was every bit of F O I N E! He had skin the color of hot caramel. His lips were on the smaller side. However, they were full and as pink as a strawberry Starburst. He stood at least six feet and was built. This man looked as if he stayed in the gym daily. He could bench press me. That's all I know.

"You must be Kori?" he asked, snapping me out of my

trance. I was so into checking him out, I forgot why I was standing there.

"Huh?"

"You Rizz's cousin, right?" he asked with his eyebrows raised. For a minute, I had to think about who he was referring to. I didn't know Paris by Rizz, nor did I call her that.

"Yeah, and you're Lah? Right?" I was praying I remembered this man's name correctly.

"Yeah. Come on." He waved me inside the club. As I prepared myself to follow him inside, the bouncer, who'd been quiet the entire time, had the nerve to whisper.

"Well, I guess we know who's dick she's sucking." He snickered to fat ass, otherwise known as *Donald*. Donald didn't even look dude's way. I guess he was good at taking orders because he hadn't said a thing since Lah came outside.

Walking into *Club 8*, I was mesmerized by the scenery. The entire vicinity was decked out in white with touches of gold everywhere, everything from the drinks to the balloons were white or gold. There were bottle girls prancing around in all-white suits with gold ties and stilettos. I knew their feet had to be hurting, for real. Nevertheless, they kept smiles on their faces and continued to serve the guests gracefully.

"Thank you," I smiled, taking a flute of champagne off the tray as one the girls stopped in front of me.

Lah led me up some stairs and into another area where everybody was dancing, drinking, and just having a good time. Like myself and pretty much everyone in the club, they were sporting white with some touches of gold.

Everyone seemed to have white attire and gold accessories.

"Koriiii!" Paris stretched my name as soon as she saw me.

I all but ran to her. I was so happy to see my cousin. She looked so gorgeous, and her glow was phenomenal. If I didn't know any better, I'd assume this was her party and not the birthday guy, who I was excited to meet. Paris spoke so highly of him and his family.

Born and raised in Portland, Oregon, I didn't get to spend much time around her until I was in my junior year of high school. My mother and her father were brother and sister. While my mother and I lived in Portland, she and her father, my uncle Pierre, lived in Chicago.

From what my mom told me, she was born and raised in Chicago, then moved to Portland after meeting my father, who shall remain nameless. I never met him.

She said that she'd gotten pregnant with me and was so hell bent on keeping up with my dad. Anyway, that didn't work out because he was nowhere to be found. I'd asked my mother about him a few times and she just brushed it off. I asked her if my dad didn't want her and she had no family in Portland, then why not move back home? She explained that she was ashamed. The guilt ate at her so much, she just stayed away, building our new life in Portland.

Apparently, Uncle Pierre was 'that nigga' because he found her and tried to make her come home. Stuck in her ways, my mother wasn't budging. She'd built her life in Portland and wasn't departing from it. Uncle Pierre, knowing his sister, let it go. However, he made a promise to keep us well taken care of. He'd kept that promise.

Because of my uncle, I could go to college worry free. I attended PSU (Portland State University) for my bachelor's in mass communications. After, I headed straight to Chicago to attend school, majoring in marketing and minoring in art design.

I had a little hobby in drawing and painting. Besides reading, it helped keep my mind on the straight and narrow. Anytime I was stressed about anything, I'd begin to doodle whatever came to mind first. It usually consisted of whatever I was irritated about.

"Hi, cuzzy!" I sang as soon as I was in her embrace. I could tell she'd had more than a little bit. I smelled whatever she'd been drinking on her breath on contact.

"I'm so happy you made iiitt!" she slurred, adding a little dance with it.

"Me too, boo! I needed this. Thank you for inviting me."

"Oh, no problem boo! Your graduation is in a few weeks, right?" She pointed at me with her eyes squinted and head cocked to the side. I had to giggle at her because Paris, my big cousin, was lit!

"Yaass, cuzzy!"

"Ayyye! Let me get a round of shots over here for the graduate to be, please!" She put her glass in the air and twerked a little.

Joining her, I popped my booty like I was a stripper at Magic City too. I was with my favorite cousin and about to graduate with my master's. Who cared if I got a little loose? I'd pay for it in the morning.

"Ayyye, fuck it up, Rizz!" Another woman, who I had never met, joined our twerk session.

"Ayyye!" I laughed and chanted, twerking a little harder.

"I know y'all not getting it in without me!?" Another woman, who I had yet to meet, joined us as well. The two women who joined us were gorgeous.

Once the song was over, we all caught our breath. We stopped just in time. The shots had come. Grabbing two each, we all clinked our little glasses and threw them back one at a time.

"Whew!" I gasped, feeling the burn slither down my throat.

As I said, it'd been a good minute since I had a good drink. The most I drank was a glass of champagne here and there. That was only in the bathtub, though.

"I'm sorry Rizz rude, boo. I'm Liz and you are?" The light bronze-skinned, shorter of the two women held her hand out to me. Taking her small soft hand into mine, I shook it.

"Hey, I'm Paris' cousin, Kori. Nice to meet you."

She offered a warm smile before kissing the back of my hand. "Nice to meet you too, love."

If I wasn't mistaken, this girl was flirting with me. Rizz must've noticed my vibe because she slapped Liz's hands off mine. "Cut it out, Liz!"

"I just be playing. Dang, sis." Liz cracked up. I looked between the two of them with a confused face. I was missing the point. Was this girl gay, bi, or straight and just playing to be funny? "I'm sorry, boo. I was just playing with the whole kiss thing. I hope I didn't make you feel some type of way."

"Oh no. You're good, love." I coyly smiled. I wouldn't

dub. Liz was fine. However, I didn't swing that way. I gave credit where it was due, though.

She had medium light brown skin, was an inch shorter than me, and was petite. She was dressed in all-white pants, a gold bandeau, and a white blazer. The fact that she wore sneakers instead of heels told me she had a different style. I was feeling her vibe. It screamed 'turn up' but 'chill'.

"I'm Iyanna, you can call me Yanna, though. It's nice to meet you, Kori." The taller, slender woman with a round bottom pulled me into a hug. "Sorry, I'm a hugger."

"It's cool." I laughed a little. "Nice to meet you, too."

"Ohh, you got to come and meet my best friend, Rell, and brothers, Isi and Lah." Rizz grabbed my hand and pulled me across the dance floor.

"And Pops, too! It's *his* birthday," Liz called from behind me.

"You know she only sees Rell when they're in the same room," Yanna joked. Liz laughed in agreement.

"I know, right? I don't see why they don't just get together and Rell could leave that bitch, Keyona, where he found her — the alley."

"Liz!" Yanna quietly exclaimed.

"Yanna! You know it's true! Don't front because Kori here." Liz was a little handsy because she slapped my ass. I jumped, but not because I was scared or acting funny. It was unexpected. I could tell Liz was going to be a handful.

"I heard that shit, Liz! I ain't that damn drunk," Paris slurred. We broke into giggles listening to her spit those words out.

I didn't know Rell like that. The way my cousin talked about him, I could tell she had a lot of respect for him.

Clearly, I was missing multiple points tonight. What Yanna and Liz said stuck to me. Was Paris in love with a man that already had a girl? If so, I had no room to judge, but at the same time, I didn't want my cousin to get her feelings hurt.

"Relly!" She might as well had run to him with the way she was jumping up and down. I thought it was funny and cute.

"Rizzy, What's up ma?" The guy, Rell, came over and scooped her up into his arms, giving her a bear hug.

From the outside looking in, you could see the love between the two. If you paid close enough attention, you could see two different types. I now knew what Liz and Yanna were talking about. While they made a bomb couple, Rell was with someone else. The overprotective side of me emerged, and I grew salty thinking about how this man had Paris all in love and had a whole fiancée sitting in the corner. From the looks of it, you could tell she didn't care for Paris.

"Relly, this is my cousin, Kori. Kori this is my best-fraann, Israel," Paris made the introductions.

"She's lying. That's her nigga," Liz jokingly whispered from the side of me. Holding my laugh in, I extended my hand out to Israel.

"Hi. Nice to meet you, Israel."

"You as well, love. You can call me Rell, though."

"Okay, Rell." I smiled as he let my hand go and placed it on the small of Paris' back.

"You introduce her to Mom, Pops and them yet?" he asked her.

"She met Yanna and Liz already," Paris replied, staring into his eyes, then she turned to me. "You met Lah too, right cuzzy?"

"Yeah. Well, kind of. He came and let me in." I rolled my eyes just thinking about the hassle I had to go through to get in.

"Was he rude?!" Before I could answer her question, she was jumping to conclusions and heading toward the table where everyone else had disappeared to. "See, I'm gon' fuck him up!"

"Paris, wait. I didn't say —"

"Islah!" she cut me off, screaming his name as we got closer. "Lah!"

Oh Lord. Her drunk ass! I thought to myself.

"Fuck you calling my government and shit for, Rizz? Fuck you want, acting like a fed?" he all but yelled in her face.

"Bump all of that. You disrespected my cousin, Lah?" Paris sized him up, going chest to chest.

Rolling my eyes, I tried to cut in. "That's not what I —"

"The fuck? Hell no! I let her in like you asked." Again, I was cut off, this time by Lah.

"Mhm, yeah, okay. Don't make me fuck you up, Lah! You know I will." She poked him in the chest. He looked at her finger with a grimace. For a minute, he was mean mugging her pointer like it owed him some money and had been dodging his ass.

"Rell, you need to get your girl. Rizz drunk ass know what's up. I'll slap her silly ass."

Paris was about to slur something else out her mouth. That is, until Rell wrapped his arm around her waist and pulled her away.

"It's nice meeting you, little sis. Looking forward to your big day."

Hearing him say that, I was moved. Paris must've been

talking me up. When I turned back around, Lah was still standing there with a grimace on his face. I felt the need to apologize for Paris' behavior since it was causing confusion.

"I'm sorry about that. I wasn't trying to start nothing,"

"You're good, shorty. Rizz was out of line. She never comes at a nigga like that." He sucked his teeth.

"I feel you. She's just drunk. Please don't be upset with her, Islah."

"How you know my gov?!" he barked, completely disregarding what I said.

"I heard Paris call you that when she came over here."

"Did I give you permission to call me that shit?" he rudely asked.

Scrunching my face up, I looked at this man crazy because he had me fucked up. I didn't know him and vice versa. He didn't have any right talking to me out the ass. Now, I regretted apologizing for Paris checking him. This asshole deserved the shit.

Licking my lips, I prepared to tell him about himself. "First of all —"

Before I could get another word out, he casually walked away. "Aye, Pops!"

He was now standing with an equally handsome man. He looked a little older, but not too old. I knew, for sure, he was much older than I. If I was seeking a sugar daddy, he'd be a contender.

The two men stood there talking and laughing like nothing else mattered. Lah was cool as a cucumber with the guy, as if he didn't just come for me a little under a minute ago.

Next, a woman with a neck length bob came over and

hugged the older guy around the waist. She was beautiful! To me, she looked blasian (black and Asian).

Her eyes were slanted and almost closed when she smiled. She had silky Nutella skin. The way her hair was set up, I knew it was real. Her baby hairs were laid!

I continued to watch Lah stand there with the couple. The way they stared into each other's eyes, I could tell they were in love. It was touching. It was like no one else mattered in the world but them. A smile creeped up on my lips watching them share a kiss.

Lah caught me staring and glared at me. Rolling my eyes at his ass, I matched his mug. In return, he cut his hard as fuck at me.

Bitch ass, I said in my head. I didn't care how fine he was. If the nigga had a nasty attitude, he might as well have been hideous.

I didn't give a fuck how fine shorty was. I wasn't with the attitude she thought I was going to stand there and take. Nah, she had the wrong nigga. Islah Perez Casique wasn't that nigga. Using my pops as a getaway was some smooth shit. Now, shorty was over there looking just as stupid as Keyona's bitch ass, sitting in that corner alone.

Keyona, man, I didn't fuck with that bitch. Shit was mutual because the whole time she been here, she ain't speak to nobody. Not even my pops, whose birthday it was. What kind of disrespectful shit was that?

Rell could've left his dog at home. He could've at least gave the bitch a command since she only moved when he told her to. I bet money he told her ass to 'stay' while he went and handled Rizz ol' drunk ass.

Rell and Rizz, though, that was a different story. Everyone but them saw that they wanted each other. I didn't see how they could be so blind.

Even though Rizz had pissed me off with the way she came at me, that was big sis. I loved her, and I knew the feeling was mutual. Hopefully, Rell was getting her together so she could come back and apologize to me. I wasn't kissing ass or disregarding shit this go around. Drunk or not, Rizz was wrong.

"Islah!" once again, I heard my gov being called and got irritated. Turning to see who it was this time, I fixed my face and posture.

"Hey, ma. What's up?" I bent over to hug my mother.

My mama was a tiny thing. She was also a certified savage. She carried a lot of respect in these streets. I'd seen her do some unthinkable shit. When niggas heard her name, they knew. Bitches envied her, though they'd never jump.

She was the only woman who could break a nigga down and have me in my feelings. Other than that, I was putting these broads in check. This was Ma, though, and I loved her to death. When you saw her, you knew she was the wife of Perez Casique. Pops didn't play about his family. At an early age, he taught us that is was *us before anything*. That meant if it wasn't family, it didn't matter. He always said that all he wanted was for his family to stick together.

That's why when Rell called himself straying away, we had to get him back. Wasn't no bitch about to have bro's vision clouded. Pops told us the biggest downfalls in this game were pussy and money. Niggas loved bitches. Pussy packed power, so when they fell, they fell hard. Niggas also loved money. Would do anything for the right price. Pops taught us to never let a bitch get you, and don't let money define you. It was all about family, love, and loyalty with us.

If I said Keyona was ugly, I'd be lying. Shit, I could see

how Rell got so deep. This bitch was fine. She was thick and petite. In other words, 5'5 with brown eyes with a winning smile. I didn't know how good her pussy was. Had to be grade A. Bro been putting up with her for two years now. That's explanation enough.

"Where are your brothers and sisters? It's time to sing happy birthday to your father."

"Isi and Yanna are on the dance floor hugged up. Liz is with them, probably getting her groove on. Rell and Rizz went somewhere so he could calm her down. Ma, you know she came for me?" I called myself low-key snitching. Ma wouldn't do anything, though. Rizz was more like a daughter to her than anything.

"Mhm, did she now? Well, what you do to my baby?"

My face fell with a fake hurt expression. See what I mean? Rizz was *her baby*. "I ain't do nothing, Mama."

"Mhm, Islah, sure." She smirked with an eye roll. "Okay, well could you please round everyone up for me so we can sing happy birthday to your father?"

"I got you, Ma." I gave her a kiss on the cheek. She thanked me and went back to sit on my pops lap.

Standing there watching, I got caught in watching them. That is, until they started kissing and groping each other. To have parents who were still in love as the day they met was a blessing. To me, it was a sign. like there was love out there for everyone — even a nigga like myself.

As of right now, I wasn't with that love shit. No, I didn't have no sad ass case like a bitch set me up or she cheated on me. I just wasn't ready. It was as simple as that. I'm twenty-four and enjoying myself as far as being single.

I could come and go as I pleased. I didn't have to answer to anyone, and I loved the shit.

Even though I was coolin' it for now, I knew the day would come when I'd want a family of my own. You know, a wife, kids, maybe a black lab. The whole shebang.

Other than my parents, Isi and my sis in law, Yanna, were living proof that people still loved hard. They'd been together since Yanna was in college. I didn't know the exact story. That was for them to tell. I just knew they were a dynamic duo — a power couple. I admired that shit. If ever I decided to settle down, I only prayed it was half of what them and my folks had.

Making my way to the dance floor, I spotted my siblings. Isi and Yanna's cute asses were damn near making love on the dance floor. Liz wasn't standing too far away as she grinded her ass all up on some Young MA lookalike.

No one was for sure if Liz was gay or not. Half of the time, she swore she was playing. Then, there were times when we'd catch her doing gay shit, like slapping or squeezing female's booties. I didn't know if she'd gone the whole nine yet. Time would tell on her ass.

"Ayo, Ma said it's time to sing happy birthday to Pops." I stood at a good distance so they could all see and hear me. There was no need in me repeating myself. Scanning the club, I didn't see Rizz or Rell. "Where Rizz and Rell?"

"I don't know. I haven't seen them in a grip. Rizz is lit as fuck though," Isi cracked up. I joined him in laughter. Word was bond. Rizz was tore up. You could tell her ass hadn't had a good drink in a grip. The way she was guzzling when she stepped foot in the spot, it was obvious.

"I know where they at. They somewhere fucking." Liz laughed.

She was bent over, throwing her ass back. The stud chick leaned back with her tongue wiping her top row of teeth. This bitch was cheesing harder than Mr. Clean.

"Liz, get yo ass off her!" I all but snatched her off the stud.

"Aye, why you cock blocking, yo?!" Young MA's twin called herself getting in my face. I didn't tolerate disrespect like that. Female or not. If you were big enough to step up, you were big enough to get it.

"Yoo, like you really need to back the fuck up off me."

"Let my girl go."

"Girl!?" Isi, Liz, and Yanna's asses all exclaimed.

"Yo, you heard what the fuck I said. Let. Her. Go." She pressed her little ass titties against my chest. She had her teeth gritted like that was going to move me somehow.

"Aye ma, you ain't doing shit but turning me on. Back up off me before I have to handle you." I kept my tone even. There was no need to turn up on her. That shit was for the birds. Actions spoke louder than words, feel me?

"Is that a threat, nigga?"

Without speaking another word, I grabbed her arm and twisted it. I now had her turned to where her back was against my front. As she struggled, I leaned down and let my words caress her ear.

"We could've been cool. You wanted to take me there. I'm going to let you go. I don't want to hear shit else from you. Now, run the fuck along."

With that, I pushed her into the crowd. She fell to the

floor, taking two other females down with her. I didn't stick around to see what happened next. Grabbing Liz by the hand, I led us back to our section. Isi and Yanna had already made their way over. They were sitting next to Pops and Ma, on the same lovey dovey shit.

"Damn, Lah. Why you had to do her like that?" Liz whined with her bottom lip poked out.

"Do what? I told shorty to back up off me. She thought she was big shit. Had to bring her down a notch. Who was that clown anyway?"

"Her name is Shane. I met her on the dance floor before you came over there." Liz didn't hesitate to tell me.

"Who invited her?"

"I'm not sure. I didn't even think to ask that. Had to be one of the other associates." She shrugged like it was nothing. See, that shit wasn't sitting well with me. Liz knew better than that.

She'd better be glad it was me who grabbed her and not Pops. I was even surprised Isi didn't say nothing. He didn't play when it came to shit like that.

"You was feeling her or something?" I slightly smirked. She was trying hard to keep her smile from emerging. Her facial muscles were working against her because baby sis was grinning so hard, my cheeks hurt and turned red for her.

"She was cool or whatever. I wasn't ready to jump the broom, though. I can't get with her now anyway. Not after what just happened." She shook her head, turning to look at me. I knew what she was doing. She wanted me to give her the green or red light with ol' girl.

It'd been like this since we were younger. If I wasn't with it, Liz wouldn't be either. This was my road dawg, fa'real. We had each other's back growing up since we were closer in age.

Liz and I were so close, we shared a room at one point. The funniest shit about that, we had a big ass house and everybody could have their own room. Liz wasn't having it, though. When she was little, she'd come and sleep with me. It was like that until she eventually started moving her shit in.

"I'm not blocking, sis. I'm just saying. I ain't feeling her. Do what you want, though." I left it at that. Watching her closely, I could see the wheels in her head turning. She was weighing out her options and debating on giving the stud chick a chance or not. Suddenly, something came to me. "I thought you said you weren't gay?"

"I'm not gay," she replied with a straight face.

"So, you bisexual then?"

"I wouldn't call it that either." She shrugged.

"Then what you call it, genius?" I asked sarcastically with a 'boo-boo the fool' look on my face.

"I like what I like." She bit her bottom lip, looking off in another direction. Following her gaze, my eyes landed on Kori. She was on the dance floor, stealing the show. There was a good crowd on either side of her, just cheering her on.

"Damn," I whispered under my breath. I couldn't dub. Shorty was fire, and she could really move too.

The way her body snaked to the beat had me in a bit of a trance. Chris Brown's song "Drown in It" was pouring all over the club. The way the song mixed with her body movements, I had to move around a little. If not, I might've been caught on hard.

"Let me go get her so we can sing happy birthday." Liz started to prance off in that direction.

"Nah, let me go get her ass." Moving my hand in front of her to halt any more of her movement. She sucked her teeth and pushed against me.

"Why you cock blocking, Lah?"

"Nigga," I had to laugh.

"I'm serious, Lah. I got my eye on her," Liz said in a dead ass tone. Scoffing, I waved her off.

"You stick to Sane or whatever the fuck ol' girl's name is." Leaving her standing there, I went to go get Kori's fine ass. Shorty had a little mouth on her, but I couldn't deny her.

Part of the reason I moved away from her earlier was her eyes. They were deep brown and penetrating. The shit was creepy. It was like she was staring into my soul. Then, she had some cute ass, small but thick lips. If I was a creep nigga, I'd eat them off her face. I also liked the way her hair went past her shoulders. I was a sucker for chicks with long hair. There was something about running my fingers through that shit. Her length fit her face too, It was round and cute. Other than that, she was an inch taller than Liz, being 5'6 and a little on the skinny side. I mean, her titties looked like they were just developing, and her ass needed a little more grip. Shiiet, give me a few months with her, I'd have her thickened in all the right places.

Moving through the crowd, I made my way to the middle where she was. There was a mixture of weed, alcohol, and cologne mixed with sweat lingering in the air.

"Aye, ma," I tapped her on the shoulder to get her attention.

She stopped dancing, looking at me with a mixture of shock and irritation on her face. "What?"

"Come sing happy birthday to my pops."

"Hmm, was that a demand or request?" She placed her hand on her chin like she was thinking.

"It's whatever you want to call it. Come sing happy birthday to my pops." I kept my tone the same. I didn't have to yell to get my point across.

"No," she flat out said. "Say please first."

"Ha! Shorty, you buggin'." I laughed out loud.

"*It's whatever you want to call it.* Say please first." She looked me square in the eyes.

She was low key rocking back and forth. It was like she was trying to keep her balance or something. I guess that drunk shit ran in the fam. All I know is if shorty showed her ass, I was going to give her what Rizz's ass didn't get. No apologies or nothing.

"One…two…three…four…fi —" I began to count and she got in my face, cutting me off.

"Six, seven, eight, nine, ten! Shit, I can count too —" I was finished talking as I picked her up and threw her over my shoulder. "Islah! Put me down!"

She was kicking against my chest and beating on my back like a mad woman. I swear, her ass was being extra. She had damn near all eyes on us.

Smack!

I slapped her on the ass, moving through the crowd. "I told your ass to come sing happy birthday. You had to test a nigga's patience."

Smack! Smack!

"Then, you go and keep spitting out my government name and shit. Strike two, ma."

"Nigga, if you don't put me the fuck down! You don't know me to be tryna tell me what the fuck to do!" She continued to beat me on the back.

"Stop hitting me. If I hit your ass back, you ain't gon' like me," I calmly warned.

"I already don't like you!" She continued to beat me in the back.

I'm not going to lie. Feeling them baby ass punches low-key turned me on. I could only imagine how it would feel to have her scratching my shit up with them claws she called nails.

"*Happy birthday to you...happy birthday to you...*"

Fucking around with her hard-headed ass, the fam had started singing happy birthday to Pops without me. I wasn't the only one, though. Rell and Rizz weren't back yet. Placing Kori on her feet, I turned her around and held onto her so she wouldn't get too far. I had my arms wrapped around her stomach and waist. She tried to fight me as I held her tighter.

"Stop fighting and sing before I have to handle your ass in front of the fam."

"I don't give a fuck what you h —"

"Sing," I hissed in her ear. At the same time, I grasped her soft little booty and massaged it. I added a little pressure each time my hand would go down. By doing this, I was sending electrical shock waves to her pussy. She'd frozen up and stopped talking shit. Still, I didn't hear her singing.

"Sing." I squeezed harder.

"*Happy birthday you, happy birthday to you, happy birth-daaay!*" she joined the fam as they sang the last part. Once the song was over, I let her ass go.

I knew she was a mixture between shocked and wet. She was also aroused and most likely wanted more. If she learned to act right, I might break her off a piece. Until then, I wasn't fucking with shorty like that.

By the time everything was said and done, Rell and Rizz's ass still weren't back yet. By now, we knew they weren't coming back. I mean, Rizz was pretty messed up.

If anything, Rell was making sure she was straight. I'd bet my last dollar that he was sitting on her couch, massaging her temples until she fell asleep. Rizz had done it for him many times before, so of course, he was going to return the favor.

Rell and Rizz, man, I wish they'd just say fuck the bullshit and be together already. The whole fam was rooting for them. Anytime you brought that shit to Rell, he'd swear up and down there was nothing there. Yeah, that was a load of bullshit and he knew it. You could see Rizz had feelings for him from a mile away. Stevie Wonder could even see that shit man. I wasn't mad at Rell for being there for big sis. I was irritated at the fact that he agreed to be the designee and left all our asses — including Keyona.

She'd kept her stuck up ass in the same spot all night, didn't participate in singing happy birthday, nor did she interact when it was time to open gifts. This was her opportunity to try and get along with the fam, and she missed out on it. If she wasn't going to do it for herself, she could at least do it for Rell.

"Sooo, an Uber it is then, huh?" Yanna was talking to Isi as he massaged her big booty.

Yanna was my sis and all, however, she was fine as fuck. She put me in the mind of a thicker version of Meagan Good. I couldn't help but stare at her sometimes. It never went as far as me fantasizing about her, though. That was some old dirty bastard type shit. I just thought baby girl was fye.

"Rell's ass knows he's wrong for leaving us like this," Liz complained, standing next to me.

"He's handling Rizz. I hope she cool," Isi called out before burying his face back in his wife's neck. Yanna's ass just giggled like a schoolgirl. Cute asses.

"Well, I hope it was worth it." Liz smirked. Just then, Keyona walked up with her hands on her hips.

"What was worth it? Where is Israel?!" She demanded to know.

None of us looked her way. It was simple. We didn't speak to that bitch. Shit, she didn't speak to us. When she did, it was always on some fake shit. It was like she was rehearsing the lines Rell scripted for her. None of us could see how he was staying with her. Then again, it wasn't for us to see. I guess, 'love's a bitch'. Shit, I don't know. I'd never been in love. When I did fall in love, I prayed I wasn't so far up her ass I couldn't see or smell the bullshit.

"Fuck it. Let's just call an Uber. He with Rizz for the night. We ain't gon' hear from his ass 'til morning." I knew Liz purposely pointed out Rell's whereabouts.

Out of all of us, she despised Keyona the most. Her biased ass was so stuck on wanting Rizz and Rell together that she didn't see him with nobody else.

"Oh, he's with *that* bitch." I wasn't staring Keyona's

way, but could tell she'd cut her eyes when she referred to big sis. Closing my eyes, I did a countdown from five to one.

"Bitch!" Just like I knew she would, Liz swung around. Baby sis was ready to fight.

If I was a messy nigga, I'd let her do it. Film the shit and everything. Since I wasn't cut like that and Keyona was Rell's bitch to handle, I grabbed Liz the fuck up.

"Chill, sis. Act like this bitch been doing with us all night. She ain't here."

"Ughhh!" Liz started punching the air like she was Ronda Rousey on a good day. The shit was pretty comical too.

"Liz, chill out, ma." I laughed. Isi and Yanna joined in on the laughter. Liz was jumping up and doing punch-kick combos, like the Mortal Combat characters.

Kori came out of the club with her phone glued to her ear. For some reason, I got a little irritated. I didn't know who she was talking to, but I wasn't cool with it at all. I'm just saying, I just felt her up and she was already talking to another nigga?

"Hey cuzzy, I was just calling to make sure you're okay. Call me back when you get this. I love you, goodnight."

"She with Rell. She's cool. You won't hear from her until the morning," I notified her once I figured out that she was talking to Rizz's voicemail. She continued to stare down at her phone, not paying me any mind. I had the right mind to snatch her ass up by the collar for not acknowledging my ass.

"Shit," she hissed under her breath. I watched as she put her hand on her forehead and closed her eyes. She was doing that leaning shit again. It must've been from all the drinks she consumed. Next thing you know, a cab pulled up in front of her. The driver's window came down and he called her name.

"Kori Bryant?"

"Yes, that's me." She went and got in.

"Where to?" he asked just as I opened the car door and slid in. Kori was too busy staring me upside the head to answer the driver.

"What are you —"

"Give him your address." I demanded in a cool demeanor. She looked at me like I was crazy. I bet I had this girl's head gone by now. I did and said what I wanted, by any means, and she couldn't do shit about it.

"Look Islah, I don't know who you think you are. I'm not about to play this game with you. Can you please get out my car?"

"The last I checked, this wasn't your whip, and cabs hold more than one passenger at a time."

"Well, this one is taken. Please get out."

"Nah, I'm staying. Driver, start going. Run her shit up until she gives you a destination." I only said that because the way Kori was set up, she was petty as fuck. She wouldn't tell him where she stayed unless I got my ass out the car. That wasn't happening, so he might as well make some money in the process.

"Sir, please don't do that. He's leaving. Islah, get out!" She shouted in my face. Our faces were so close that I could smell the liquor on her breath.

"Drive." I slid the driver a stack. His eyes lit up and that nigga took off.

"Oh my gaawwd!" Kori was spazzing. "Help! Help! I'm being kidnapped!"

"Child lock this shit." I gave direct orders to the driver. Hearing the click of the locks, I knew he followed orders. Shit, I'd just given the nigga a stack. I'd follow directions too.

"*Hellpp! Heellp!*" Kori continued to bang on the windows. Shorty was wasting her time because the windows were thick and tinted. No one could see or hear her.

I was sitting in my seat cool as a cucumber, checking my phone for any new messages. I had one from Liz. She was asking where I'd gone. I shot her a message to let her know I was good. Next, I had a message from Pops. He was reminding me of the meeting I had with the new marketing consultant he wanted to hire. Rolling my eyes, I deeply sighed.

Apparently, he already guaranteed her the job. He just wanted me to meet with her and go over what kind of exposure our companies needed. Aside from distributing some of the finest white girl in the US, we had a slew of businesses. Of course, they were all cover ups. They were legit and successful cover ups though. eventually Pops wanted us all to retire and we run our legit businesses full-time. Truth be told, we could've been retired. Our family was so set, our kid's, kids, kids, and grandkid's kids, kid's wouldn't want for nothing. The Casique family was wealthy and solid.

Pops never stopped working. Even on his birthday, he was talking about some work shit. I knew what I had to get done in the morning. He was supposed to be on his way to the Virgin Islands with Ma. It was a part of the birthday gift we all pitched in on. I didn't reply to his text.

If I did, he would just go on and on about this and that. He needed to chill and enjoy his vacation.

Feeling my phone vibrate against my thigh, I knew it was Pops. I ignored the shit, though. As soon as it stopped, it started back up.

"Pops."

"Let me find out you're ignoring a nigga and I'll fuck you up myself, Lah!" Pops yelled in my ear.

This nigga was wild. He had a crazy temper. The shit was ridiculous. The only one of us who inherited that shit was Isi. You couldn't tell because he was always so cool. Once you pissed him off, it was over. The only person who could calm him down besides Ma was Yanna. She put him at ease. She was his calm, just like Ma was to Pops.

"Pops, you on vacation. Enjoy that shit."

"Shut yo ass up!" He laughed into the receiver. Pops was always cool as fuck. The nigga was like a father/best friend to all of us. Long as we kept it a buck, he did the same. "Do what I said, Lah. I know you. You like to play games. You forgetful as an elephant too."

I looked at the phone before putting it back to my ear. "I think you're losing it, old man. Elephants have the best memories."

"Shut up. That's a damn lie. It's dolphins," he corrected me. "That's beside the point. Do what I said, Lah. I'm not playing with you."

"I heard you, old timer. Nine in the morning, sharp." I nodded in reverence to the meeting.

"Help me, please! Your son has kidnapped me!" Kori's ass was all up on my arm, trying to yell into the phone.

"Get back!" I held her in a tight grasp. As she fought in my embrace, I massaged her booty the same way I'd done inside the club, only it wasn't working as well as it did in the club.

"Who is that?" Pops sounded like a mixture between amused and confused.

"That ain't nobody. I have to go, Pops. Enjoy that gift I got you." I laughed.

"Fuck you and that Viagra! Love you!" He laughed, then hung up before I could give a response.

"Let me the fuck go, Islah!" Kori continued to fight against me in the back seat of this Lyft. The driver kept looking from the road to us in the rearview mirror.

"Aye, watch the road homie," I barked.

"Is-Islaaaah!" Kori was fighting me so good.

I placed my hand under her skirt and massaged her pussy through her panties. From the feeling of the material, I could tell she had on laced panties. Massaging deeper, I could feel how soaked her panties were.

Yeah her ass wants the kid, I smirked as I thought to myself.

"Q-quit play-inggg!" She screeched, now hevily panting. Pulling her panties to the side, I plunged two fingers inside her stickiness. That only made me hard for her.

"Islah..." she lowly whimpered, her eyes rolling to the back of her head. "Quit playing."

"Do this feel like playing, ma?" I slowed down and sped up some more.

Her pussy was so juicy, I wanted to stick my tongue in it. No lie, I never ate pussy. I felt like that should be reserved for your wife. I haven't found her yet, so I wasn't doing it.

"Mmm," she began to moan and rock back and forth on my fingers. I knew this shit was feeling good to her. I pulled my fingers out her pussy right before she could climax.

"Nooo, why you stop?" She straddled my lap and started to grind. I had this sly smirk on my face because I knew she'd be begging for more. Shorty was acting like she didn't want a nigga. Reality was, she'd been wanting me to fuck her since I made her ass sing happy birthday to Pops. I was about to give her exactly what she wanted too.

"Come sit on this dick," I demanded in a calm tone. She didn't say shit as she did what I said.

Feeling her soft little hands wrapped around my big dick, I rocked up. She lifted herself up, positioning her tight pussy on the head. The liquor on her breath kissed my nose due to her panting. My shit wasn't even in her yet and she was already out of breath.

"Sshitt!" she screeched as she slid down my pole.

"Fuck," I hissed. She was tight as fuck, but her pussy swallowed my dick whole. Feeling the pressure from the grip of her muscles, I had to readjust myself so I wouldn't nut prematurely.

"Laaah! Ohmigawd, fuck mee!" She slowly bounced on my dick.

I was squeezing her hips and bouncing her on my dick like a basketball on a court. Grabbing her titties, I pulled them out and showed each one some tongue action.

"Ahh, I'm about to cuuum!" she screamed.

"Do that shit then, ma," I whispered in her ear.

She tightened her southern muscles and slammed down once more. This caused us both to let go of our built-up nuts.

"Shit..." She fell against me to catch her breath. I caught a glimpse of the driver staring at her ass through the rearview mirror and mugged him. He saw me see him and focused back on the road.

After a few minutes went by, she gave him her address and got herself together. It was silent for a little until she said, "I hope you know that dick is mine now." She looked at me with a dead ass stare. I scrunched my face up, looking at shorty like she was straight crazy.

"The fuck?" She had me confused with some other nigga if she thought that.

"Yup. Play with me if you want to, *Islah*." She kept her act up. I honestly thought it was a joke until she grabbed my dick through my pants. I popped her hand away as the car came to a stop. I knew she was tipsy, so I didn't pay her any mind.

Before she could get out the car, I snatched her ass by the neck and planted a kiss on her lips so deep, I knew she'd be wet and try to invite me in. Once I let her go, I looked deep into her dark brown eyes.

"I call the shots."

She couldn't even say anything as she got out the car and walked her sexy ass toward her house. Yeah, I was about to keep my distance from her little ass.

CHAPTER 4
RELL

I was laying on Rizz's couch when I heard her get up and go in the bathroom down the hall from her bedroom. I was on alert in case she had to throw up. I would be right there, holding her hair and caressing her back while she spilled her guts out. After hearing the toilet flush, I closed my eyes again. Suddenly, the light in the living room flicked on and I was blinded. I had to put the pillow over my face to keep the light from burning my eyes.

"Good morning, beautiful. Are you feeling better?"

"What are you doing here?" She asked in a groggy tone as she came to sit on the couch. She was wearing nothing but the t-shirt and panties I had changed her into.

"You got drunk as fuck, so I brought you home, ma." Sitting up, I stretched. I hadn't gotten but a little bit of sleep. I wasn't all that tired. I was too concerned about her to sleep anyway.

"Oh my gosh, Rell!" Rizz's eyes bucked like she was

43

having an epiphany, like she'd just had a vision like *That's So Raven*.

"What?"

"Did my cousin ever get inside the club? I vaguely remember her telling me she couldn't get in."

"Yeah, she got in. That's when shit hit the fan. You went off on Lah. About what? I don't know. Then, I snatched your ass up and took you outside to get some air. You started throwing up and shit, so I got you in the car to take you home. On our way here, you threw up all over yourself, the seats, and a little on me."

"Oh my — I'm sooo sorry, Relly! I'm embarrassed as hell." Rizz covered her face in shame and hung her head.

"It's cool, Rizzle," I referred to her by one of the nicknames I'd been calling her since we were kids. She called me Rello, Relly, Rezzle or Rell. It was just something we'd come up with as pet names. Though they didn't have special meanings, everybody else didn't see it that way.

In school, everyone swore me and Rizz were more than friends when really, that's all it was. Could I see myself with her? Hell yeah! I also cherished our friendship more than anything. Rizz was my right hand, my go-to with *everything*. I swear, I relied on this woman for any and everything. If she wasn't in my life, it'd be dull and complicated.

"I hope you don't mind that I showered you and changed your clothes." I sat up, catching her attention.

"Nigga, please. How many times have you gotten drunk and I had to do the same for you?" She gave me a knowing stare. Lightly chuckling, I looked away. She was right. Rizz had seen my ass butterball naked too many times to count.

This was different, though. I got to see her ass naked this time. I can't lie like the shit didn't have my wood saluting her. I was a complete gentleman, though.

"You right." I nodded and looked towards her. She was staring at me with a small smirk.

"I know I am, punk ass," she laughed a little. The room grew silent for a minute. "I'm hungry. What time is it?"

I picked up my phone off the coffee table to catch the time. I saw that I had several missed calls from Keyona and my family. Shit, I wasn't even thinking about their asses. My main concern at the moment was Rizz. I had to laugh my ass off because Liz was straight going in on my ass. She was saying a bunch of shit about how she was going to fight me for leaving everybody. She also said that she pretty much ran up on Keyona for calling 'her sis' a bitch.

Off bat, I knew who Keyona had called a bitch. To say it didn't move me was a damn lie. I hated how disrespectful she was toward Rizz. Despite the mutual feelings, Rizz tried her best to get along with Keyona for my sake. She was always trying to invite her out, trying to include her and she never — not once in front of me — said anything bad about my girl.

That was one of the main reasons I loved Rizz so much. She put other's feelings before her own. I didn't know what she was saying about Keyona when I wasn't around, nor did I care. My main thing was, she respected me enough to know not to say shit in my face.

Don't get it twisted, though. Rizz did make a point to tell my ass that I could do better. She didn't come across savage about it but expressed her concerns. She said she wanted the best for me and nothing else, just as I wanted the best for her.

To me, though, no nigga was good enough for my best friend. I guess I was just scared that when and if she did get a nigga, we wouldn't spend that much time together anymore. I'd just gotten back on good terms with her. I didn't want to have to lose my best friend all over again.

"What's so funny?" Rizz asked, taking me out of my thoughts.

"Man, Liz crazy ass. She so stupid, yo." I cracked up.

"Oh Lord, what lil' sis do?" Rizz joined me in laughter. She didn't even know what Liz said or did, but was cracking her ass up. It was always some bullshit with Liz.

"You don't even want to know." I shook my head and wiped the corners of my mouth. If I told Rizz that Keyona was disrespecting her name while she wasn't there, it'd be on. I already knew. It was best that I didn't say anything at all.

"I'm hungry. Let's go to the diner. I want some break-fast." Rizz whined, laying her big ass head on my shoulder.

When we were kids, I used to always tease her about her head. She was insecure about it, and I found it funny. Back then, I was a knuckleheaded kid with no goals or morals. Anything was funny to me. Now that we were older, Rizz had grown into her head — her body, period. She used to be flat chested, no booty, and twiggy. Now, when I looked at her, I couldn't believe how far she'd come. Let's just say milk did the body good. That mixed with working out, and she was gorgeous.

"Yeah ma, let's do it. You want to eat there or take it to

go?" I side eyed her, already knowing the answer. It was simple, there was no answer. Rizz was indecisive as fuck when it came to making simple decisions like this.

"Let's just see when we get there." Rizz gave me a sneaky ass smile. I shook my head but agreed.

"Bet."

After we both were dressed, we decided to take one of her cars because mine smelled like vomit. I had all the windows down, so hopefully it was good in the next few hours.

We ended up taking the food to go. I was thankful because I didn't feel like sitting in that cold ass diner. I was trying to go back to the house, eat, chill, and go back to sleep. I planned to sleepover again. I wasn't looking forward to going home. I knew by how many times she called and texted, Keyona was on one. I left her in the club with my family, so I knew what I had coming when I went home.

"Ohhh Relly, let's watch The Lion King! It's on Netflix." Rizz spoke in a conniving tone. She was trying to get me to watch it because it was her favorite movie.

"Hell no. You always cry when that nigga Scar kills Mufasa."

"I do not!" she shrieked.

"You do too!" I mimicked. "Look at you, about to cry now," I joked.

"Whatever fool. We're watching it." She sucked her teeth and got up.

We were sitting on the living room floor, smacking on

our food. I'd ordered a breakfast sampler. This shit had everything you could think of for breakfast on it. Eggs, bacon, toast, pancakes, French toast, grits, potatoes — you name it.

Rizz ass ordered some strawberry French toast. It came with bacon and cheese eggs. While she was getting the movie set up, I stole a piece of bacon off her platter. I tried to do that shit quick as hell so she wouldn't see me. It was too late because she turned around just as I swiped it.

"Your ol' greedy ass! As much as food as you got on your plate and you go and steal mine!"

I laughed with a mouth full of bacon and pancakes. I couldn't even say anything because her ass was right. She also allowed me to do it. No matter what we were eating —breakfast, lunch, dinner — I'd pick off her plate. I used to try that shit with Keyona and almost lost a pinky. I ain't tried it with her ever again. I didn't believe muthafuckas needed three tries to learn one thing. One time, and you couldn't get me to do the shit again.

"I hope your uglass chokes too!" she cracked up, taking a seat next to me.

"That's not nice, is it?"

"Who said I was nice?" she challenged. She was now cutting into her French toast. "I'm surprised you didn't mess with my strawberries and whipped cream."

"Save me some. I was coming for that next." My greedy ass rubbed my belly.

"Oh gosh!"

"Don't act surprised nigga, and next time, I get to pick the movie."

She side-eyed me with a smirk. "Who said anything about next time? You'll be sleep before me."

"You want to bet?"

"My new Benz for your new Audi." She rubbed her hands together.

"That's petty shit. You could just buy you one. I was thinking you have to do all the paperwork Pops left for us at the office." I raised my eyebrows. Now, that was a *real* challenge.

I could get the shit done. However, it'd take forever and a day for me. Rizz could get through it in an hour and be ready to do the next thing. My best friend was a human calculator. She ate numbers for breakfast, lunch, and dinner. That was one of the reasons she went to school and became an accountant — a damn good one at that.

Pops had put her on to look after all the business funds and his and Ma's personal accounts. Whenever he met with anybody to give or receive money, she had to be there like a damn lawyer.

"It sounds like you tyring get out of doing some work." She giggled, throwing her head back.

"Shut up, big head. You in or nah?" I held my hand out for her to shake.

"Bet." She shook on it. At the same time, I reached over and scooped some of her strawberries and whipped cream onto my fork.

"Ugh! I cannot stand you!" She playfully mushed me in the side of the head.

"I know ma, but you love me, right?" I looked her in the eyes. For a minute, I got lost in her almond shaped sandy brown eyes. They were sandy brown and shaped like almonds.

My eyes traveled down to her perfectly soft and plump lips as she said, "I do love you, Israel."

I didn't know if it was the way she said my gov or the way her lips looked saying it. I moved in, without a second thought, and kissed her lips with passion. I could feel the resistance she was putting on at first, yet she gave in.

She placed her hand on the back of my neck, pulling my face closer and kissing me deeper. I could tell she'd been waiting for this moment when she parted my lips with her tongue. Now, I wasn't big on swapping spit, however, with her, I was cool with it. It was like I craved it, almost.

She pulled me on top of her, and I fell between her legs like I was supposed to be there. The shit was like a magnetic force, pulling us into each other. The warmth coming from her inner thighs and womanhood felt good, like it was summoning me in. As we continued to kiss and grind against each other, she began to deeply moan.

I pulled away from her to catch my breath. "What are we doing?"

"I don't know, but it feels right," she spoke with lust filling her voice and love in her eyes.

"We shouldn't be doing this." I shook my head. All these thoughts were rushing my mind, but still, I didn't move from the position I was in. Rizz was right. This shit felt right. Like a long time coming. She was breathing hard as hell as she stared back up into my eyes.

"We should stop, but I don't want to."

"To be honest, I don't either." I leaned down and pecked her lips. "We got to, though…"

"I can't explain the way I'm feeling, Israel. This feels good…it feels right. What does this mean?" Her eyes watered up, and a lone tear fell from the side of her eye.

I didn't know the answer to her question. Shit, I wanted to know the same thing as she did. Even though it was wrong to continue what we were doing, I couldn't stop myself. It was like a call that I had no choice but answer.

Gently, I kissed her tears away one at a time until I didn't see them anymore. After, I began to move down her body, starting at her neck. I made sure and gave both sides special attention with kisses, sucking and gently nibbling. Moving down to her collarbone, I licked across it. She let out low moans. The whole time, she held my head, massaging my scalp and the back of my neck. I can't lie, the shit felt good as fuck.

"Make love to me, Relly. Please, I want to feel you," she damn near begged through whispers and moans.

I continued to move down her body, making my way to her belly button. Grabbing her platter, I took a strawberry with whipped cream. I fingered the lining of the leggings she wore and she lifted her hips and buttocks off the floor for me to pull them down. Staring eye to clitoris with her pussy, I placed the strawberry and whipped in my mouth, then placed my mouth over her pearl.

"Ahh, Rell…"

I listened to the sound of her cooing my name like a broken record as I continued this sweet assault on her luscious pussy. She was squirming, pulling my head in and then pushing it away, then pulling it back in. I was enjoying the taste of her nectar and the feel of the fingernails as they clawed at my scalp. She'd cum three times, if not more, by the time I was finished servicing her womanhood with my tongue. Coming up for air, I noticed her eyes her slightly closed.

Moving back up her body, I placed multiple kisses on her lips, cheeks, and forehead. Rizz's ass was knocked out, snoring on the floor. I had to laugh because I knew she would be sleep before me. I just didn't expect it to be in the way that it happened.

CHAPTER 5
KORI

Waking up with a pounding headache, I had one eye opened and one eye closed. My alarm was going off, making it no better for my headache. When I fully got my eyes open, I noticed the time. I had slept thirty minutes past my wake-up time. Shit!

I was supposed to be up at seven in the morning to be at this meeting by eight-thirty. There was no way I'd have time to prepare myself on what I would say, take a shower, and be on time. At this moment, I felt like my life was over. Anybody graduating with my credentials dreamed of a job being lined up before graduation.

I hadn't even received my degree, yet I managed to land this big-time client. He offered me half a million to sign on with his company for a year. If I decided to stay, I'd be paid another half a million. Of course, I had to make sure I did my job so well that their clientele tripled yearly.

Even though I hadn't met him in person, I sent in my resume. I was listed on this website where people could inquire on marketers and bid on the best. The thing I found weird was that I was new — fresh. I made sure and explained everything on my profile so people knew ahead of time. I wasn't, in any shape or form, trying to get over on anybody.

By the time I'd finished getting dressed and doing everything else that consisted of me starting my day, it was 8:15AM.

Damn, I thought as I was patting my hair. Realization set in that I hadn't made an appointment to get my hair done for Saturday. I made a mental note to make an appointment as soon as I could find a stylist. Since moving to Chicago I'd been doing my own hair. I usually kept it up in a bun or just flat ironed it and left it hanging past my shoulders. Since my graduation was coming up, I wanted it to look cute. Plus, I was taking pictures two days before graduation.

"Where to?" the cab driver asked as soon as I slid into the back of the car. I wasn't sure how late I was going to be, so I decided to take a cab.

"The Mirabella."

I'd never been or even heard of the place. However, that's where the meeting was being held. As we drove through downtown, I admired the landscape. In some ways, Chicago reminded me of Portland.

The high-rise buildings, and some of the neighborhoods were somewhat built the same. They had this project-based community built in the hood called Cabrini Green that sort of reminded me of what we called The Ville in North Portland. The funny thing is, both projects were located on the north ends of the two cities.

"We're here." The driver announced as he pulled up in

front of the building. From the outside looking in, it appeared to be nice. I wasn't sure if this was a restaurant, hotel, or apartment complex. It could've been all three in one. The building was big and tall from the outside.

Once I got out the car and walked in, I got a better look for myself. Nice was an understatement. This restaurant was off the chain! It had cream white and gold glass marble floors. There was a crystal chandelier hanging above the entrance. To the left was an entrance for a restaurant. To the right were elevators. I looked up to see that there were thirteen floors.

"Hello, ma'am," the woman behind the big desk greeted me as I approached.

"Hi, I have reservations here." I was talking to her but staring around in awe. How could I not know about this place?

"Okay, sure. What's the name?"

"Casique."

"Let me take a look for you." She smiled at me and then went to typing on the Mac in front of her.

"Is this like a hotel and restaurant?" I asked, still looking around in awe.

"No, ma'am. It's a residence with a restaurant and open bar on the first floor," she let me know.

"Oh wow. How much is rent?" I inquired because now I wanted to move right on in.

"Girl, five thousand a month." Her real accent came out. I thought it was funny because she had this professional white girl voice going on before. Now that I asked about rent, her true colors came out. Her tone was like she wanted to say, *"oh hell no, mmnt mmnt girl!"*

"Each floor holds two three bedroom, two and a half

bathroom penthouses. The top floor is one full penthouse though. It had five bedrooms and four and a half bathrooms. Then the sixth floor holds a boardroom and a fully equipped workout room."

"Lawd hammercy." I dramatically fell against the desk. There was no way in hell, heaven or earth I was paying that much for rent. I didn't care if I had it or not. That was just too much.

"For real, girl!" She giggled a little. "Okay, right this way. Mr. Casique is waiting on you."

As soon as she said that, I pulled my phone out my bag to see the time. Damn, I was five minutes late. I was kicking myself because I was almost on time. Getting caught up in the beauty of this place, I lost track of time.

"Right this way." we stepped off the elevator and onto the sixth floor. Moving to the side, the woman let me inside the boardroom.

Again, my mouth dropped. This room was beautiful. You could see the entire city from the huge window that touched from wall to wall. The walls were different colors, and there was a big conference table in the middle of the room. As I walked further into the room, there was a man standing there with his back turned. He was wearing fitted designer jeans, designer shoes, and a plain shirt to go with the outfit.

Taking initiative, I began to introduce myself. "Hello, Mr. Casique. I'm Ko—"

"You're late." He cut me off before I could tell him my name. I felt butterflies rumble in my stomach. I knew I was going to catch hell for being late. Shit, I'd be pissed too if I was paying half a million to someone who didn't show up on time.

"I know and I apologize, but —" Again, I was cut off.

"But nothing. Time is money and money is time." He stated as he turned around. My mouth dropped when I realized who he was. He looked equally surprised, but his jaw was clenched shut.

"Islah—"

"Your services are no longer needed. Please see yourself out, Ms. Bryant." He kept an even tone with not a trace of emotion on his face.

"What?!" I exclaimed. I knew I heard him right, but I couldn't believe he was dismissing me.

"I'm not going to repeat myself, Ms. Bryant."

"Islah, I was only five minutes late. What's the big issue?" I took a step closer to him.

"Please, leave or you'll force me to call security."

"Security!? Nigga, don't act like you don't know me!" I was pissed. He was standing in front of me acting like he didn't just have me riding his dick in the back of a cab.

"Security," he called out, his voice raising an octave.

It was crazy to me how he didn't yell, yet he wasn't exactly quiet about it. Just then, two big dudes rushed into the room.

"Yes, boss?" they spoke in unison.

"Get her out of here," Islah gave the order, and they moved toward me.

"Don't touch me!" I slapped Steve Wilkos' fat ass twin, Donald's, hand off me.

"Aww look Greg, she's mad," he laughed heartedly.

"I swear for God, Islah! I hope something bad happens to you!" I pointed at him like Ms. Celie did Mister at the end of *The Color Purple*.

"Get her out," was all he said before he turned back around to whatever he was doing before I walked in.

⌘

"Oh my gawd! Are you serious, boo?" Paris asked with concern written all over her face. I was sitting on my couch with her on Facetime. I'd just told her what happened an hour ago with Islah. She was just as pissed as I was.

"Yes, Paris! I'm dead serious! He just kicked me out like I ain't mean shit!"

I broke down crying. I hated that I was crying because of this man. It wasn't so much about him as it was the way the nigga treated me in that boardroom. I couldn't understand it. How could he be one-way last night and another this morning? Yeah, he was rude last night, but I felt a connection in the back of that cab — or at least I thought I did. Now, I felt stupid as hell.

"Don't cry, baby. It's gon' be alright. I'm going to get Rell to beat his ass." She was trying to soothe me, but it wasn't working.

"No! You don't need to go bringing others into this. It's whatever, Paris. I'm over it." I sniffled and swiped the last of the tears. I didn't need her to go telling Islah's brother on him. That would make the problem bigger.

"Nah, you shouldn't have told me nothing if you didn't want me to handle it." She sucked her teeth, rolled her eyes, and looked into the camera with an annoyed expression.

"I didn't tell you for you to handle it. I told you because you're my sister and I had to get it off my chest. Please, don't tell Rell nothing, Paris. Please?"

"I ain't making no promises." She sighed, patting her weave. The way it moved when she was scratching it let me know it was loose.

"Whatever. Let's go get our hair and nails done together. I need to focus on graduation," I reminded myself more than her.

"Oh! Yaas! That's what I was going to tell you. I go to this shop call *Pretty Lady*. My stylist is the bomb. She'll have you hooked up for your graduation."

"Yaaass!" I did a little twerk on the couch. After changing out of my pencil skirt suit set, I put on some boy shorts, a tank top, and took off my bra. I liked to be comfortable in my own home.

Just then, I heard somebody else chant, "Yaaaas girl, like, for real!"

To me, it sounded like a man disguising his voice like a female. I looked all up into the screen to see who it was. "Who was that?"

"Girl, Rell's big head ass just got here. I have to go. He won this bet last night, so I got work to do. I love you and we'll link soon." She sent smooches into the phone. I sent some back. Rell did as well.

"*I love you, cuzzy!*" He still had his voice disguised. Me and Paris were cracking the hell up. He was too much. I could definitely see why they were best friends. They both were looney as hell.

"Oh gawd. Boy, get out my camera!"

I watched them go back and forth for a few more seconds before disconnecting the call. They were too much. I could say, though, they got me out of my funk. I no longer cared about Islah's ass or the way he did me. I did feel bad a little. I told him I hoped something bad happened to him. My mother always taught me to never wish bad on people. It didn't matter what they did to you or vice versa. You kept a smile and let God handle the rest. Thinking of her, I realized it'd been a little while since we talked.

Ding Dong

Right as I was scrolling for her number, my doorbell caught my attention. I was wondering who it was. Other than my cousin, my best friend, Shanah, had a key to my place.

I met Shanah my first year at Chicago State. She was funny and cool to be around. We hit it off instantly. I found it weird, but dope because I didn't really click that well with females. In Portland, I kicked it with the guys or by myself. Females were too messy for me.

"Who is it?" I called from the other side of the door.

Silence.

Sucking in a breath, I placed my hand on my hip and shifted my weight. "Who is it?!"

I hated when people wouldn't announce themselves before I opened the door. First, they showed up unannounced. Second, it was rude. Third, I didn't know who it was to be opening the door. Finally, I got tired and went to open the door.

"I said who—"

The rest of my words were stuck in the back of my throat. I was staring into the eyes of Islah. I had so many emotions running through my body as he stood there with a smug smirk. I wanted to cuss, yell, slap him, and some more stuff. I also wanted to jump on him, rip his clothes off, and fuck him into oblivion. He was standing there looking good enough to eat. He still had on the same clothes from when I last saw him, only now, I was more focused and admired how good he looked. The only difference was that he was wearing a Bulls snapback. I liked how he wore it facing forward instead of flipped backward. That told me a lot about him.

"What are you doing here? How do you know where I live? What do you want!?" I stood in the doorway, bombarding him with questions. I was wracking my brain to figure out how he could've gotten my address. I know I didn't put it on the site, even though that was an option. Was he on some crazy stalker shit?

"First," he put his finger up. "Don't yell at me. I ain't yelling, am I?"

"Fuck you," I hissed, but didn't yell.

"We'll get to that in a minute. Move so I can come in," he calmly demanded. The fact that he didn't yelled irked me. Most men raised their voices to get their points across. He was calm and assertive. The shit scared me.

"Why should I let you in after how you did me?"

"You right. You shouldn't let me in," he agreed. Now, I was a little confused.

"Huh?"

The next thing I knew, he was picking me up with ease and coming in. I wanted to start fighting this nigga so bad. However, I let him carry me inside. Once he put me down, I glared at him. I had so much pent up energy that consisted of ill feelings for him.

"Damn, you look like you want to fight a nigga." He went and took a seat on the couch. He kicked his shoes off and placed his feet on the table. "What you got to eat up in here? I'm hungry."

"The hell? Nigga." I slapped his feet off my table. I was

looking at him like he was a true psycho now. Not only did he just bombard my house, he had his feet on the table and was asking for food. *This is some light skinned nigga shit. Chocolate men have more respect than this.*

"Why are you here, Islah?" I folded my arms over my chest.

"Because I choose to be. Why haven't you gone to fix me something to eat yet?" he retorted. I looked at this man like the true nut he was. How do you show up to someone's house and demand them to make you something to eat?

"I don't want you here!" I stated aggressively.

"If you didn't, I wouldn't be sitting on your couch right now. Just like I didn't want you in that meeting. You left, right?"

I shifted my weight and rolled my eyes when he said that. "Speaking of which, why did you do me like that?"

"You know the answer to that question. Am I going to have to make my own food?"

"Yup! But you're not making it here. Get out!" I pointed to the door.

"Have you seen that movie yet? I have it on DVD. I'm going to bring it next time I come over," he said while putting his shoes back on. I couldn't deal with this dude. It was like he didn't care about anything I was saying. The shit was irking my soul.

As he stood to his feet, his body towered over mine. He reached to chin-check me, but I moved out his way.

"Leave! Now, Islah!"

He stood there staring at me for a few more seconds. It was making me feel uncomfortable. We held eye contact until I broke our intense stare-down by looking away.

After that, he walked out the house, leaving me to stand in the middle of the room.

Once the door was shut behind him, I rushed to lock it. He must've still been on the porch because next thing I know, I heard him laughing crazy. Yeah, this nigga was nutty. I had to keep my distance.

CHAPTER 6
RELL

Keyona: *Where are you???*

      Keyona: *Why haven't you been home, Rell???*

Keyona: *Did you forget we were supposed to meet with the wedding planner this afternoon???*

Those were all the questions Keyona just texted me. Closing my eyes, I palmed my face and blew out a frustrated groan. I completely forgot we were supposed to see the wedding planner today. I forgot all about the fact that this wedding was in motion.

Lately, my mind was in other places. I was trying to wrap my mind around what went down between Rizz and I a few nights ago. It was crazy because I was feeling some type of way about her and didn't know how to deal with it. All I knew was, the shit felt kind of good.

As we sat in my father's office, I watched her diligently work on the paperwork my father left for me to do. I focused on the way her hair hung in her face. The way her eyes would dart from one end of the paper to the other.

Even the way she was holding that company pen was sexy.

Keyona: I know you see my messages!

Keyona: Don't ignore me, Israel. You really don't want these problems, boy.

Moving the phone away from my face, I had to side eye the messages. Keyona had been talking to me off the chain lately, like she was asking for a fat lip or black eye. I never placed hands on her or any other woman. With the way she'd been coming for me, she was pushing my buttons.

"Done," Rizz spoke. I looked from my phone to her.

"Damn, girl. That was fast." I acknowledged her and went back to my phone. I was trying to figure out a nice reply to my fiancée.

Me: Bitch! Who you think you talking... *backspace, backspace, backspace* I'm at the office right now. I'll hit you when I'm finished.

That was the best she was going to get. I wanted to say more, but left it as that.

"What's wrong?" Rizz touched my arm. I could've sworn I felt chills go through my body. It was like an electrical shock wave.

"The usual." I sighed.

"Oh, okay. Well, was that all that Pops left behind?" She looked at her watch like she had somewhere to be.

"Yeah, but I wanted to talk."

"Okay. What's on your mind?" She gave me her full undivided attention.

"So, about what happened between us..." I didn't know exactly what to say about it. My mind was still on how good she tasted on my tongue.

"What about it?" She smiled with a shrugged.

"What was that about?"

"I don't know. What do you want me to say, Relly?" She shrugged once again.

"Say how you feel, Rizz. Help a nigga understand what's going on with us, shit." I chuckled a little.

"I mean, there's not much to say. You ate me out. The shit felt good. It felt...right." She looked toward the ceiling, then back to me. "We're best friends and it shouldn't have happened. I mean, you're engaged and I'm seeing someone that I really like."

"Seeing who?!" I stood up without warning. Rizz jumped in her seat and scooted back in the chair. She was looking up at me with a look of fear.

"Rell, chill."

"The fuck you mean, *chill*?" I barked. I didn't know what it was. I couldn't calm myself down. "You didn't tell me about this nigga. When you meet him? How long y'all been seeing each other?"

"Rell, why are you trippin'?"

"Answer me, Rizz!" I couldn't hide my annoyance or keep my voice down, for that matter. I didn't give a fuck who was in this office. The way the offices were set, shit was soundproof anyway.

"First of all, you need to sit the hell down and calm yourself. You're acting crazy! I don't know what you're going through with Keyona, but you—"

"Whoa, back the fuck up. This ain't about Keyona and you know it. You trying to take the light off you," I called her bluff. Rizz was dead ass afraid to tell me who she was dealing with. Then again, she could've been feeling guilty because she hadn't told me anything about it.

"Even if that was true, I don't have to tell you anything, Israel."

"Oh, it's like that?" I stood again. She just gave me this look that said she wasn't for my bullshit. "That's fucked up, Rizz. Since when do we keep shit away from each other?"

"Rell, please, don't. Who I'm dealing with shouldn't matter one way or another to you!" She stood her short ass up. We were now toe to toe, face to chest. Even with heels on, Rizz was short.

"That's a bunch of bullshit and you know it!" I pointed down in her face. She swatted my hand away and took a step closer to me. Without warning, I picked her up and sat her on the desk.

"Rell," she breathed out in somewhat of a moan. She was pushing against my chest and the shit was turning me on. Pushing her back against the desk, I laid my head against her chest. I was smelling her scent and rubbing my face against her skin.

"Rell, please..."

"Please what, baby?" I bit her nipples through the silk shirt she was wearing. I couldn't help it. They were calling out to me. They wanted to be sucked and licked by a real nigga. I was going to be the one to do it.

"What are we doing?" she asked in a serious tone. However, she was moaning too.

"I don't know, baby." I gave her the truth as I reached my hand under her skirt and rubbed her pussy lips through her panties. She was so fucking wet, she was soaking through the panties. Opening her legs further for me, she began to grind against my fingers. I slipped my hand inside and inserted two fingers inside her pussy. I was working her juices and pressing against her throbbing clit.

"Sss...Rell, oh my gawd!" She was now playing with her nipples and riding my fingers.

"That feel good, baby?" I sent a trail of kisses down her neck and chest. It was taking everything in me not to rip her shirt off. If I did that, all the buttons would pop off and her ass wouldn't have anything to wear. She'd be forced to walk out of this office in nothing but a bra and blazer.

"Yaaass," she yelped, grinding harder. Watching her suck and bite her bottom lip had my shit on hard. I couldn't take it anymore, I had to feel her on my dick.

Pulling her off the desk, I switched places with her. I had her between my legs, giving her slow and sloppy tongue kisses. I put my hands under her ass and lifted her onto my lap. She was grinding as we kissed. The next thing I knew, she undid my jeans, placed her small hand inside, and pulled my dick out. I was turned on by the sight of her licking her lips. She was damn near drooling as she looked at my shit. Lifting her skirt over her plump ass, I ripped her panties off. We were now in a position where her womanhood was kissing the tip of my dick. Slowly, I eased her down on to it.

"Ssss," she winced in pain at first. Soon, she was moaning in pleasure. I had to keep myself from howling out like a dog. Rizz had the tightest pussy I'd ever been inside of. It made me wonder if she was getting dick in her life, or if she ever had dick.

"Damn, girl," I hissed as I rocked against her while she rode me.

"I'm about to cuuum!" she hollered out as she bounced. I stood up with her still locked on my manhood.

Sitting her on the table, I spread her legs wider and readjusted my girth inside her. This caused her pussy to open up a little more for me as well. Rizz began to finger her clit as I gave her long, thick strokes.

"Oh gaaawd! Rell! I'm. about. To. Cuuum!" She let go all over my dick. I was right behind her.

"Cum, baby," I leaned in closer and whispered in her ear. Just like that, she was squirting, wetting up the bottom of my shirt. I was right behind her within one stroke.

"Damn," Rizz breathed out. I was out of breath my damn self. Leaning down, I rested my head on her shoulder and buried my face in her neck. She smelt so damn good in my arms. I hadn't even moved out of her. She felt that damn good. "Rell?"

"What's up, baby?"

"Do you have feelings for me?"

Thinking about her question, I couldn't answer that question for real. "I don't know."

I felt her stiffen under me. "Move."

She was trying to hide it, but I heard the break in her voice. Backing up enough to look her in the eyes, I could always tell when she was about to cry, and now was one of them.

"What's wrong?"

"Nothing, just move." She roughly pushed me away.

I stood there looking dumbfounded as she was slipping her panties and shoes back on. "Rizz. Talk to me. What's up?"

"Nothing, Israel. Just leave it alone, aight?" She strutted past me to go get her purse and blazer from the desk.

"Where are you going?"

70

"Dude, can you back up? Give me some fucking space, damn!" She pushed me.

She now had big tears rushing down her face. "Rizz—"

"Rell…" She took a stance and pointed in my direction with evil eyes. "Just, give me some space."

With that, she walked out of the office with a hard switch. I just stood there wondering where I went wrong.

"Hellooo…earth to Israel!" Keyona waved her hand in my face.

"Huh?" I shook my head, snapping out of my thoughts. I couldn't shake Rizz for the life of me.

"I been calling you for the last five minutes." She rolled her eyes.

"Aye. What I tell you about that eye rolling shit, yo?" I grimaced. See, now we were face to face and not over text message. She wasn't about to be talking to me crazy. I'd yoke her ass up before anything.

Clearing her throat, she softened her voice a little. "I'm sorry, baby. I was just trying to get you to look at these samples."

Looking at the photobook she was holding, I admired the colors. Everything was silver and a cream white. The only problem I had was how much all of this was going to cost. It wasn't like I didn't have it. However, I wasn't trying to spend no more than I had to on this wedding. I gave Keyona a two hundred and fifty-thousand-dollar wedding budget. She should've been able to get the wedding of her dreams together with that.

"Everything looks nice, bae. How much is all this costing, though?"

"Umm..." She looked into space like the answer was chilling there or something. She wasn't slick. I knew exactly what that meant. She wasn't keeping track of the budget. She was just running the black card up without a care. Knowing her ass, she was all up in the malls with it too.

Raising my eyebrows, I looked at her for answers. "Umm is not an answer, ma."

"Okay, baby. Don't get mad, but..."

"But what?" I deeply sighed, palming my face.

"I saw this other cute wedding gown and I had to get it. Then—"

I abruptly cut her off before she could say anything else. "Whoa, what the fuck? You got like four already. How many do you need, Keyona?"

"Oh, so I'm Keyona now? It's like that, Israel?" She folded her arms over her chest and pouted.

"Answer my question. Stop trying to distract me." I raised my voice an octave.

"Now you're yelling at me?!" She burst out into tears. I looked at this woman like she was insane. Here it was, I was trying to get to the bottom of why she needed so many dresses and she was flipping shit, crying and shit. "Baby—"

"No, Israel! The wedding is off!" She jumped up and ran toward the back. We were sitting in the shop of the wedding planner. The wedding planner was sitting across from us. She stared at me with an evil glare. Look, I didn't know this bitch, nor did I care about her eyeballing my ass.

"Fuck you looking at? I pay you to plan a wedding, not gawk in my business." I mean mugged her ass and got up to go find my fiancée.

Real shit, Keyona was starting to work my nerves with the way she was acting. It was this wedding, I swear. She was never this way. She was usually chill, laid back, and fun to be around. I had to get to the bottom of why she was such a bitch now.

"Baby, open up the door." I knocked on the bathroom door.

"Go away, Israel!" She sounded like she was crying.

"Baby, let me in. I'm sorry," I pleaded outside of the door. "Baby—"

Just then, the door flung open and she stood there with her arms over her breasts. Her weight was all shifted to one side and she was glaring at me.

"What's the matter with you?" I asked, walking us back into the bathroom and closing the door. I didn't need anybody, especially the nosey ass wedding planner, all up in our business.

"You!" She poked me in the chest.

"What am I doing wrong now?" I asked, dryness following my tone.

"Everything. I don't know what's going on with us anymore. You not coming home. You're staying at the office later and later. Then, you always yelling at me over little shit. It's like you're treating me like your child and not your future wife. What happened to us being partners in this relationship? Huh?"

I hung my head, listening to everything she was saying. Part of it was true, while the other shit was false. She was right about me staying at the office late. We were in the middle of a huge transition. I had to put in more work than a little bit. As far as me yelling at her and treating her like a kid, shit. If she would act like an adult, then she could get treated like one. Not only was she extra whiny. She was irresponsible as fuck when it came to certain things — like money for instance. I mean, look. I gave this girl a budget and she already went over the shit.

Like always, I recited my famous line. "I'm sorry, baby. You're right about everything. I need to do better. Tell me what you want me to do, and I'll do it."

As of lately Keyona wasn't happy and neither was I. If I'm being honest, I wasn't too sure about our relationship anymore. I stuck it out because of the time we had put in. I kept telling myself things would get better between us.

After what happened with me and Rizz, that's all I could think about. I felt like shit for making my baby cry. I hated that I couldn't face my true feelings for her. well, I could, but I always kept them hidden. Rizz was my best friend. Us taking it beyond that would ruin us. Wouldn't it?

CHAPTER 7
KORI

I was sitting in my car, scrolling through the email I had just received. It was from this local business owner named Kassidy Kyle. She owned an event planning service. Her email explained that she was trying to get more clients to hire her for their events. She'd been in the game for three years and business was slowing down. She was offering me five thousand a week for a month. If things took off for her, she'd keep me around.

Going into business for myself as a marketing consultant was tougher than I thought. Not only did I want to prevent my time from being wasted, but I also didn't want to waste their time either. Receiving this job offer, I felt a little better. It made me think about my mama. She always said, "*Baby, when one door closes, another opens.*"

At first, I was discouraged due to how things went with Islah. Now, my confidence was up and I was feeling like I could do this marketing shit. I was just excited to give my clients some pointers about how to grow their businesses. Seeing others happy always made me happier, so this was the perfect job for me.

Tap, tap, tap!

"Heyyy, bish!" my best friend, Shanah tapped on the passenger side window. I was parked in front of the shop Paris had told me to come to, *Pretty Lady*.

From the outside looking in, it seemed legit. I'd seen several women go in and come out with smiles. Either they had their nails, brows, or hair done. I was going to need all of that.

"Hey, boo!" jumping out the car, I rushed to give Shanah a hug. Since she was graduating as well, I figured she'd want to get done up. This was also an opportunity for her to meet Paris.

Shanah was in school for journalism and communications. She'd already landed a job with the Chicago Tribune as a copy editor. She was working her way up to be a reporter. I couldn't lie. At first, I felt some type of way because she got a job off bat while I was still struggling to get something simple. Then again, I wasn't that pressed. I chose to work for myself. She was working for someone. In my book, it was always harder to work for someone else.

"Man, I'm so excited about Saturday! I pray I don't sweat my bundles out too much tonight."

"What? Tonight? What's happening tonight?" I was all ears. I needed something to do tonight anyways.

"Oh, girl, I'm going to this new club. It's called *Good Vibes Only*."

"Who you going with?! I want to go!" I was jumping up and down like a kid on Christmas that just got everything they wanted.

"You can come. My cousin, Shane, and her girlfriend are going to slide through as well." she informed me. Before I could say anything, I spotted my cousin's red beamer pulling up.

I smiled, admiring how pretty Paris was. Growing up, I always admired my cousin. She was so beautiful and always had the best of everything. While I could've had the same things, my mother wouldn't allow it. She was dead set in her ways, so much that she wouldn't let my uncle move us back to Chicago, where she was originally born and raised.

"Hey, cuzzy!" she greeted with an open hug.

"Hey, boo! This is my best friend, Shanah. Shanah, this is my cousin, Paris."

"Hi!" she waved. Instead of waving back, Paris pulled her into a full hug.

"Sorry, girl. I'm a hugger. You gon' have to get used to it."

Watching my two best friends laugh and interact made me feel good. I had a feeling they would click, even though they were from different sides of the Chi. Just then, I spotted two other cars pull up. One was a brand-new Range Rover. The other was an all-black Audi with tinted out windows. I watched as Yanna stepped out of the Rover and Liz got out of the Audi. Yanna was dressed casually in jeans and a short-sleeved shirt. Liz, on the other hand, was dressed down like a tomboy today. Her hair was bone straight and hanging past her shoulders and down her back underneath a Bulls snap. She was wearing makeup with matte nude lips.

"Hey, ladies," I greeted them upon approach.

"Hey boo." Yanna hugged me.

"What's up gorgeous. You miss me?" Liz's flirtatious ass hugged me and tried to grope my ass. I slapped her hands away and pushed her off me.

"Oh Lord, I ain't dealing with you today." I giggled. Liz was fine and all, but I wasn't like that.

"Too late." She laughed and turned to Shanah. "And who is this? Looking all fine and thangs." Liz just couldn't help herself. It was crazy because she acted just like her brother. She was straightforward and knew what she wanted. While it was scary, it was a huge turn on.

"Shanah, this is Liz. Be careful, she might bite your ass." I laughed because Liz licked her lips and bit her bottom lip at her. From the looks of things, Shanah was enjoying the attention. Let me find out she been keeping secrets.

"Hello, Liz. Nice to meet you."

Liz kissed the front and back of her palm. "The pleasure is mine, beautiful. You got a boyfriend...or girlfriend?"

I could've choked on my spit. This damn family was just too much for me. "Really, Liz?"

"Bye blocker!" She put her hand in my face. I just stood there with my mouth agape. Paris and Yanna were both doubled over, laughing their asses off. "So, Ms. Shanah. What's up with us tonight?"

"Well, Kori and I are going to that new spot, *Good Vibes Only*. You should slide too, boo," Shanah just free and willingly told our business. Then, she extended an invitation. Like, fuck what Kori thinks. It wasn't that I didn't want to be around Liz. I just knew if she showed up, she might bring her brother. I wasn't in the mood to be dealing with Islah. I just met this man, and already, he was a problem. I couldn't lie, his dick game was amazing. If we did see each other again, it'd include me riding him.

"Ooh! We want to go too!" Paris excitedly said. She was doing a little happy dance and everything. I had to laugh because my cousin was funny.

"Yaaas! Me and Isi been wanting to check it out anyway. I heard they got hookah in there," Yanna chimed in. I smiled at her.

Yanna was so pretty to me. She had brown skin, full lips, dark brown eyes, and an oval-shaped slender face. Her nose was pointed and pierced, giving her that bougie look. She was far from that. She proved that when we met. She was shaking her ass just like the rest of us, husband and all.

"Yeah, and we can invite Lah and Rell!" Liz added, looking between Paris and me.

"No!" Paris beat me to the response. Closing my mouth, I turned to give her a certain look. Now, all eyes were on her. We were all giving her this 'what's going on' look. "I mean, he's busy with Keyona. They are planning a wedding, y'all. Or have y'all forgot?"

Liz and Yanna turned with their lips pressed to the side and noses in the air. "Mmnt."

"So, that means they need to be spending more time together than anything. I'm bringing my new boo anyway. I don't need Rell all in my business, trying to check my dude." She sucked her teeth with a roll of her eyes. Call it women's intuition, but something was telling me that she was hiding something. I wouldn't call her out now, though.

"Speaking of my brother. What happened the night y'all left us at the club?" Liz asked her. She was still holding onto Shanah's hand. Shanah didn't seem to have a problem with it. She was all smiles as she waited with Liz for Paris' answer.

"Girl, to be real, I was too drunk to remember anything. Can we go inside now?" Paris moved past us all. If I wasn't sure before, I was damn sure now. Something other than friendship was going on between Rell and Paris. I wasn't going to push the subject anymore. I'd wait until we were alone to get the truth out of her.

From the look Liz was giving her, she didn't believe her either. "Hmm, okay sis. Let's go, baby." She opened the door for Shanah.

"*Baby?*" Yanna and I asked with a hint of laughter.

"That's right. Baby, y'all hating?" Liz ass smirked at us. Yanna and I both shrugged. Shanah stood there smiling like a fool.

"Mhm, bih. You got some explaining to do!" I whispered to her with a playful smack to her bottom. Liz caught it and stopped me at the door.

"Ma'am, please keep your hands to yourself. I wouldn't want to have to handle you for my baby." She was laughing, but I couldn't tell if she was serious by her tone of voice.

"Guh," I gasped out, cracking the hell up. Liz was about an inch shorter than me, being 5'5. She wasn't a threat, by far. I wouldn't tell her ass that, though.

We were fifteen minutes into getting pampered when out of nowhere, Paris mentioned, "Oh, and I didn't tell Rell on Lah-Lah, Kori. I should've, though." She sipped on a glass of Roscato.

"What Lah do?" Yanna was getting a massage on the other side of the shop but heard Paris.

"Girl, this nigga—" Paris started to explain, and I cut her off.

I didn't want everybody in this shop to know my business like that. Besides us, there were six beauticians and two people waiting at the door. Paris and I were getting our hair done, Liz and Shanah were getting pedicures, and Yanna was basking in her massage.

"He didn't do anything that needs to be mentioned."

"Secrets don't make friends, babes. What my brother do? I might be able to help." Liz looked up from spitting game to Shanah. I looked at her with a worried look. I didn't know if I wanted her to know what I'd done with her brother or how he treated me. As I told Paris, I didn't need anybody handling him. I guess I was taking too long because Paris began to run the story down.

"Basically, Lah and Kori fucked in the back of a cab. The next morning, she had an interview with him, unknowingly. So, she showed up five minutes late for whatever reason. Lah didn't give her a chance to explain or nothing. This nigga just had her tossed out the conference room."

The entire time Paris talked, her knee bounced. She only did that when she was nervous or irritated. "Paris, chill. It's over. I got a new job offer and I'm content with it."

"See, it couldn't have been me. I would've beat his ass for doing me like that. Like, nigga you know who I am! You better than me, Kori." Shanah added her two cents. Liz was staring at her the whole time.

"Don't worry about that, baby. I'm not stupid like my brother. I wouldn't do you like that." She kissed the back of Shanah's palm. This bitch was back to giggling like she didn't just have a savage moment. Lawd, this family was off the damn chain. It only made me wonder how their parents acted.

"But don't sweat any of that, best friend. This may sound weird, but Lah likes you. He's never been great at expressing his feelings. He just going about it in a weird way. Shit, he probably was spooked at how you were the one who showed up to that meeting," Liz told me. Nodding my head, I didn't know what to say. I guess it made sense, in a sick kind of way?

"You got to get him back, though," Yanna pointed out in a matter fact tone.

"What you mean?" I was all ears.

"Girl, you have to show these Casique men—"

"And woman!" Liz cut Yanna off, looking dead at Shanah.

"Yeah, her ass too. You have to show *this family* that you ain't nothing to play with. So, now you have to get him back," Yanna protested.

"But how?" I couldn't even believe I was even entertaining this thought. I was never the gettsy backsy type.

"Ooo! I got it!" Paris tapped her feet on the black and white checkered floor. We all stared at her for answers.

"Do tell," Liz sarcastically replied.

"Okay, so you know how he showed up to your house after everything went down?" Paris asked me.

"He showed up to your house after he kicked you out the meeting girl!?" Shanah exclaimed with a mean mug. She looked like she was ready to go find Islah right now and beat his ass for me.

"Yeah, girl," I told her and then turned back to Paris. "Okay, so?"

"So, you have to do the same thing to him!" she shouted a little too loud. Paris was now on her third glass of wine.

I shook my head with disdain on my face. "No, I can't do that. I won't do that. That man will kill me."

"You ain't lying," Liz said loud enough for me to hear. My eyes bucked and head shot her way. There wasn't an ounce of laughter in her tone so, I knew she was for real.

"See," I shook my head. "I'm not about to play. Plus, it's not even worth it. I don't know him and vice versa."

"True," Shanah agreed.

"But listen, baby girl. You don't want to get involved with us Casique's unless you really about that life," Liz informed me with a serious look. I wanted to ask what that meant. Instead of inquiring, I let it go.

"Shit, ain't that the truth." Paris slurped the rest of her drink while looking down at her phone. She was only using one hand and a thumb. That thumb was moving across the screen fast.

The next thing I knew, my phone vibrated in my purse. I dug inside and pulled it out. Paris had texted me.

Paris: *The Mirabella. 13th Floor. Access Code: 3793*

Looking up, we made eye contact. Silently, we spoke to each other. I was saying, *hell no I'm not going to this man's house*. She was saying, *oh yes you are!*

Lord, be a fence because this is too much.

CHAPTER 8

LAH

As soon as I entered Good Vibes Only, I regretted coming. I swear this was a fucking setup. Not only was Kori here, two of my ex's were as well. The only reason I was annoyed by my exes was these were the two craziest muthafuckas on my roster.

Shantel and Keke used to be best friends or whatever. That is, until Shantel got with me and Keke started hating. At least, that's how Shantel explained it. I didn't give a fuck about either of them, so hell yeah, I was banging them both. Shit was funny as hell because they would come over and talk hella shit about each other to me. Shantel had me first and Keke would come, talking about some 'I saw you first, she stole you from me' shit. The stupidest shit ever, I wasn't neither one of theirs. I was just doing me, living life how I wanted, like I am now.

"Hey brother!" Like always, Liz was the first to greet me. I leaned down and gave her a hug and kiss on the cheek. "Ohh, I want you to meet somebody."

She pulled me over to where she was sitting next this

fine ass caramel skin. The club was dimly lit, but I could see her eyes were dark brown. She had thick and full lips, a medium button nose, and a winning smile. I didn't know where baby sis picked her up at, but shiet. Sharing is caring.

"Baby, this is my brother, Lah. Lah, this is my boo, Shanah," Liz made introductions. Even though I was cool with Liz loving on girls, I wasn't cool with her adding labels to them quite yet.

"What's up?" I greeted shorty anyway. I didn't want to run ol' girl away in case Liz was, indeed, trying to build something.

"Hi." She smiled. She was more into the music and hookah than anything. Beyoncé's song "Sorry" was playing. See, this was another reason I couldn't be up in this spot. It was full of a bunch of women bashing men to that fucking *Lemonade* album.

"Hello to you too, Lah!" Rizz's loud ass said from behind me. I didn't even know sis was here. I had to admit, I was happy as ever to see her.

"What's up, big head girl. You know not to call me by my gov." I playfully mushed her in the side of her head.

"Whatever! Stooop! Don't be messing up my hair either," she whined.

"*Stooop!*" I mimicked her ass.

"Ugh, you're so annoying." She giggled and gave me a hug. I kissed her on the cheek and released her.

"Where Isi and Yanna?" I inquired. When Liz texted me, she gave me a list of who all might be there. She didn't say if Rell and his tag along were showing up. That was neither here nor there.

"Yanna said she and Isi had a change of plans. They'll

catch the next outing," Kori spoke up before anyone else did. Nodding my head, I went and took a seat a few inches away from her. Real shit, she was smelling and looking good as ever. I was surprised she even said two words to me.

After what went down at the interview, I felt kind of bad. I had remembered her address, so I decided to do a pop up. My intentions were to go there and apologize, fuck her brains out, and dip. Instead, I did the total opposite. I was rude and annoying. I didn't know what it was. I felt the need to be an asshole toward her.

"So, Paris, where's your new boyfriend?" Liz asked, taking a sip of her drink. She had the rim of the glass against her lips, looking over the glass at Rizz. I laughed, knowing she was being petty. None of us called her Paris. She'd been Rizz since we were kids. I never knew why we called her that, just did.

Rizz flipped Liz the bird and rolled her eyes. "Fuck you, Liz."

"I'm just saying, shorty. You said you was bringing your new man. I want to meet him," Liz continued to egg her on. Rizz was back to sipping her drink as she lightly chuckled.

"He'll be here."

"What's up y'all?" Rell walked up unexpectedly.

"Oh, he's here now." Liz laughed her ass off. I couldn't take it anymore. I had to crack up with baby sis because Rell came right on time.

"Oh shit," I held my stomach. I got a glimpse of Kori next to me and she was laughing as well. The only one looking lost was Shanah. You could tell she didn't know what the hell was going on.

"What's so funny?" Rell inquired, looking between us all.

"*Nothing.*" Kori, Liz, and I all spoke in unison.

"Oh, what's up, Rizz? You didn't see my text this morning?" He disregarded us all and got straight on Rizz. She rolled her eyes in annoyance.

"Nah." She was lying. She got his text. Whatever the text said, now I wanted to know.

"I didn't get a text. I want to know what my text said," Liz smirked at Rell. He went over and snatched the glass of whatever she was drinking out her hand.

"The fuck is you drinking, yo?" He sniffed the glass. "Is this an alcoholic beverage?"

"*Is this an alcoholic beverage?*" Liz mimicked him. She was cracking the hell up, like it was the funniest thing ever. With the way Rell's nostrils flared and the mug on his face, you could tell he didn't find anything funny.

"It's time for you to go home. Let's go." He snatched her up. I could see why he was so annoyed. However, he didn't have to manhandle baby sis like that. Of course, I didn't say nothing about it. Shit, Rell was my older brother too.

"Rell, let her go! She chilling with us. Damn, we good. She good." Rizz stood up and defended Liz, who now looked like she wanted to cry because Rell was making her go home. Liz was barely twenty-one and just having fun.

Rell still had ahold of Liz's arm as he glared at Rizz. Whatever was going on with him was deeper than Liz getting a little tipsy. The way he was glaring at Rizz said a lot. Then again, it could've been Keyona stressing his ass out.

It was sad because even Stevie's blind ass could see he

wasn't feeling Keyona anymore. I was wondering what was keeping him with her. Then again, that was none of my business. She might've had some A1 pussy he didn't want to give up. Either way, my palms were itching for the day he left that bitch.

"Come take a walk with me. You tripping for no reason." Rizz got out her seat and pulled her dress down to cover her exposed thighs. Leave it to Rizz to wear something revealing, but she looked good in it. She made the thot wear look like bad bitch-classy chick.

Once they walked off, we went back to making small talk. It was now Kori, Shanah, Liz, and me sitting there. To be honest, I was ready to go. I was only sticking around because my sister and Rizz were there. Plus, Rizz's 'so called' new boyfriend was supposedly coming through. I wanted to meet this nigga.

"Ohh! This is my song!" Shanah jumped up and started gyrating her hips. "Kori, let's go dance! Liz, you want to dance, boo?"

"Nah, bae. You go ahead." Liz was chilling. I still found it funny how she was calling this chick bae all of a sudden. I hadn't seen her a day in my life. Liz was going to explain this shit.

"Yeah boo, let's go dance." Kori got up and followed Shanah to the dance floor. I was all eyes on her until Liz broke me out of the spell I was in from staring at her ass.

"What's up with you and my future wife?" she asked.

"Who, Shanah?"

"Kori," she confirmed with a serious look. I started laughing at her ass. She appeared dead ass.

"Man, go about your day. You know what it is with me and shorty."

"Nope, you're holding out."

"What you mean?" I laughed out loud.

"She told us what went down between y'all. Well, Rizz did, at least."

"Damn, you women love to talk, huh?" I shook my head. I bet Kori just couldn't wait to tell my sisters what I did. Knowing Rizz the way I did, she was salty about it. She hadn't brought anything up yet, though.

"That was them, bro. But get this. There's a rumor going around, saying we got competition. Like, mutha-fuckas is inquiring about our name and everything."

"Word?" I was all ears.

"Real shit, bro." She nodded with a serious look. This bit of news was shocking to me because it was the first time I'd heard about it.

"How you find out about that?"

"I overheard Isi and Yanna talking about it earlier. To be honest, I think that's where they are now."

"Where?" I sat up straight and got closer to her.

"Nigga, are you listening? People inquiring about our name. They going to find some shit out."

Now, I was mad that I was here instead of there with them. Nobody even told me. It wasn't abnormal for Isi and Yanna to handle shit together. That wasn't my issue. I just wished they would've said something to me about it.

"So, where are they now?" I stood up, waiting for her to give me some info.

"If I knew, I wouldn't have my ass here. I'd be riding the fuck out with them."

"Shit." I took a seat and placed my head in my hands. I wanted to shoot my bro a text, but decided against it. If he and Yanna were truly going to get answers, he didn't need any distractions.

"I think Ma and Pops need to come home sooner than later." She took a sip of her drink after saying that. I shook my head. I wasn't feeling that. If Pops brought his old ass home, he'd be stressing this shit. He'd be in the streets hunting for the monkey himself.

"Nah, it's best we keep this under wraps for now. Who knows? Isi and Yanna might've come up with some answers."

She shrugged. "True."

"I wonder what's up with Rell and Rizz. They been acting funny since Pops birthday," I mentioned to her. I couldn't put my finger on it. Something was off. Like, they weren't on their usual lovey dovey shit.

"I already told you. They're fucking—hard." Liz cracked up. "No, seriously. Watch, they're fucking. I promise you they are. Why you think they acting like that?"

"Man, you stupid. I know they got feelings. But fucking? Nah." I shook my head. I wouldn't believe it unless I saw it— literally.

"Aight, whatever. Don't say I didn't tell your ass." She leaned back against the seat.

"How much you want to bet?" I smirked. Looking into her eyes, I noticed Liz's eyes were transfixed on something. I followed the direction they were going and knew why.

"The fuck she doing here, Liz?" I grimaced as her little friend from Pops' party approached with Shantel and Keke on both arms.

"I don't know. I ain't spoke to her since Pops' birthday."

"What she doing here then?" I barked. I wasn't feeling ol' girl since Pops party. Man, I knew I shouldn't have come out. Then again, I didn't care for Liz talking to her either.

"You got hearing problems tonight, huh?" Liz decided to play with me at a time like this. Cutting my eyes her way, I tightened my jaw. The stud was coming over toward us.

"Well, well, well. We meet again." She smirked.

"Fuck out our section, yo." I nodded to her.

"I think you're mistaken. This here is my section. So, y'all can bounce."

"Nah, this my girl and her people's section. She invited me and my fam over to chill," Liz started explaining shit to this clown. I wasn't with it.

"Say less, Liz."

"Ha! Listen to captain save a bitch here," the stud scoffed. I honestly forgot ol' girl's name. That's how much of a nonfactor she was to me.

"I got yo bitch, bitch!" Liz's little hot-headed ass ran up and jumped on the stud. The stud was about 5'10, and Liz's little ass was only 5'5. She was always trying to fight people bigger than her. I used to kid her and say she had little woman syndrome.

"Oh, hell no!" Shantel and Keke shouted in unison.

They were now charging at Liz as she was on the stud's back, beating her in the neck and head. Apparently, she wasn't hitting hard enough because ol' girl was holding her own. The way she was moving her body to try and get

Liz off her was low-key funny. It looked like Liz was riding a mechanical bull.

"I think the fuck not." I snatched Keke's ass. I couldn't get to Shantel quick enough. She was now pulling on Liz's hair.

"Liz! Oh, hell no!" I heard from behind me. I didn't know who it was because I was focused on trying not to hit this bitch, Keke. It was sort of hard because shorty was wilding in my grasp. The next thing I knew, she was bucking and kicking while I held her under my arm. Looking up, I saw what she saw.

Kori was giving Shantel the business! Like, shorty was real life fucking it up. Like, hitting them one-two's and stomps. Shit, I know my ass wasn't about to get into no fight with her ass no time soon.

The next thing I knew, the club lights came on. A team of security rushed our section and broke the fight up. Keke's bitch ass ended up biting my wrist, and I swear I wanted to punch that bitch in her head. Security might as well have been feds. I wasn't catching a plea for her.

"Oh my gosh, Shane! Are you okay?" Liz's girl Shanah ran over to the stud. I had to give it to baby sis, she did that. That stud bitch was all fucked up. One of her eyes was swollen shut, she had blood leaking from one of her nostrils, and a fat bottom lip.

"You know this bitch?!" Liz exclaimed. She appeared angry.

"This bitch is my cousin. The one I was telling y'all about. What did you do, Liz?!"

"I did?! She came over here name calling and starting shit. I just gave her what she wanted!"

"We need a paramedic! She's having a seizure!" one of

the guards called out. All I could think was *damn*. I had to think fast, though. Pops was out of town, the cops were on their way here—shit was all bad. I had to get me and my sister out of here.

"Liz! Bring yo ass on!" I grabbed her.

"Get ff of me!" She snatched away. This wasn't a time for us to go at it. She stopped running and turned around. "Kori, let's go!"

"I'm not leaving my best friend!" Kori shrieked.

"Fuck her, shit. It's you that's going to jail if some shit pops off with the po-po!" I fussed. Liz was worried about all the wrong shit. Kori was a big girl. If she wanted to stay, so be it.

"Man, that's Rizz's cousin! We can't leave her here. Rizz gon' fuck us up!"

"Fuck Rizz too, shit! You want to go to jail or nah?"

She stopped like she was thinking, then, took off running to the exit again.

As soon as we got outside, we spotted Rell's whip. He was rolling in the Audi tonight. Just to give him and Rizz fair warning about what was going down, I jogged over there. I left Liz with my keys so she could get her little hot ass in the car.

As soon as I got to the car, I got an earful. From the sounds of things, Rell was knocking Rizz's pussy in. She was screaming and moaning his name so loud, the shit might drown out the sirens nearing us. I made a sharp U-turn and went to get in my car.

"What they say?"

"Nothing." I shook my head and took us to my crib.

Liz and I were chilling on opposite couches when Isi, Yanna, Rell, and Rizz entered my penthouse. The only thing I didn't care for too much when I moved to the Mirabella was the way the door systems were set up. Living on the top floor, I was the only penthouse up here. That's right. My shit took up a whole floor. It was that big. I had five bedrooms, four and a half bathrooms, a pool/jacuzzi outside, and a fully equipped kitchen.

"Aye, what happened at the club?" Rell was the first to ask as he took a seat on the couch. Rizz was busy pacing the floor and moving her fingers across the screen of her phone.

"This bitch we got into it with on Pops birthday started popping off at the mouth. So, I beat her ass and the bitch started having a seizure!" Liz spoke first. Her ass was standing up, all animated and what not. I immediately looked to Isi. It was crazy because if it wasn't Pops, I was looking for Isi's reaction. He was the oldest and shit. Whenever we got out of line, he was on our heads.

Liz was staring his way as well. Just like with Pops, Liz was Isi's baby. She could do no wrong in their eyes. She could've started the shit and they would find a way to justify her ass. It didn't look like he was feeling nothing she just said.

"Really, Lizzy? As much as we talk about shit like this and you go and get yourself caught up? What if ol' girl presses charges? She knows your name and face," Isi calmly spoke. I sat back in my seat because if he was calm, that meant he was about to turn up pretty soon.

"Where were y'all niggas at while my baby sister was doing all this fighting?!" he directed at me and Rell. I stepped up first to save Rell some time to gather his shit. I could tell this nigga was trying to come up with some legit shit to tell Isi.

"I was there. I was holding one of the other women back."

"Women!?" he shot up. Here we go.

"Yeah, bro."

"Rell! What's up?!"

This nigga started stuttering and shit. I had to cover my mouth so I wouldn't get caught laughing. "Um, um, I, I, was outside t-talking to Rizz."

"Oh, you were talking to Rizz, huh?" Isi asked with a slight smirk. The corner of his mouth began to twitch just a little.

"Y-yeah, man." Rell nervously looked around.

"What was so important that y'all wasn't in the club with baby sis and bro?" Isi eyeballed Rell and Rizz. Rizz hadn't looked up not once. She was busy still moving her fingers across her phone's screen. Isi looked so aggravated it wasn't funny.

"Rizz!" Isi yelled, damn near shaking the room. Rizz jumped in her stance, almost dropping her phone.

"My bad, Isi. I was trying to get ahold of my cousin. I haven't seen her since I left with Rell," she calmly apologized and explained. If it were me or Rell, she would've had a lot of lip. Because it was Isi, she had more respect for him and knew he didn't play that shit.

"See, you and Rell leaving and shit. Shit pops off. Can't do shit and leave y'all in charge. Wait 'til Pops finds out about this shit." He shook his head.

"*Pops?!*" we all sounded off in unison.

"Why you got to go and snitch to Pops?" I jumped out of my seat like it was hot.

"Come on, mannn. Let that nigga breathe. He on vacation and shit. We all safe. Nobody was shot or went to jail," Rell stressed out. I nodded my head in agreement because he was right. Shit, we were all here at the crib chilling. On the low, Kori still being out there had me a little worried, but not to the point I felt the need to go out painting the city different shades of red.

"Right, Is, you tripping for nothing," Liz took a chance and spoke up. It was in her best interest to shut the fuck up, though. Isi wouldn't take his frustrations out on her, no matter how much it was her fault.

"Man, y'all—"

"Baby." Yanna placed her hand on his chest and looked into his eyes. It was crazy because whenever she did that, he'd instantly calm down. The shit was cute, but weird. Well, to me, I found it weird. Maybe when I found the one, it wouldn't be weird.

"Aight, aight, aight. My baby wants me to calm down. So, I ain't snitching this time. However, y'all need to stay out of shit that'll disrupt the peace of our family being free on the streets." Isi pointed his finger at Rell, Liz, and me.

I was thanking God for big sis at this moment. If it weren't for her, Pops would've been on the first thing smoking. None of us wanted that. Not even Isi no matter how much his snitching ass thought he was going to tell.

Pops hadn't even been gone that long yet. Please let that nigga stay where he was. The longer he stayed the better, if I had a say in it. Not only was he a workaholic, but he was also always on our asses.

It didn't matter if we were doing right or not. Pops always stressed over our moves. Having an active father was a blessing, don't get me wrong. I just wished he would've trusted us enough to breathe and do our own thing.

As soon as we got the last shipment off, we were done. I couldn't wait. I had plans of finding myself. Since being a part of the family business occupied my time, I never truly figured out what I wanted out of life. If I did like doing anything, I could take the time to explore it. I was always taking orders from Pops, or Isi. I loved my old man, but he had no chill at times.

"In the meantime, we need to stay low-key. Meaning, no clubs for at least a week or two. Nothing too flashy popping off either. We'll give this chick a few days and see where her head at, and then we'll move if need be.

"Liz, come on. You're going home with me and Isi. Rell, take Rizz home. Rizz, I'm praying sis hits you up. Tell her we'll see her at her graduation. Lah you need to hire that marketing consultant Pops told you to. You know he isn't going to be feeling it if he finds out you been out here doing the most." Yanna was now the one giving out the orders and reading us our rights.

Everyone nodded their heads. Meanwhile, Isi was eyeballing her with lust in his eyes. You could tell this nigga was ready to rip into her right in front of us.

"Aight, we out." Rell chucked the deuces with Rizz in tow. Next, Liz was up and following Isi and Yanna out the crib.

Once everybody was out, I headed to my bedroom to shower. I had a few things to look over in the morning. At the top of the list was finding out who these niggas were inquiring about our name.

Ding!

I was asleep in my bed when I heard the elevator doors open from the front room. Everybody had left, so I knew someone was coming in. The only people who had the access code were my inner circle — my family. I assumed it was Liz or one of them that forgot something, so I stayed asleep.

Hearing the click clack against the marble floors, I figured it could only be one of my sisters, unless it was one of my brothers in dress shoes. Then again, neither Rell nor Rizz wore dress shoes. Pops did, though.

This nigga went and snitched anyway, I thought while socking the air. Getting out of bed, I prepared myself to go face Perez Casique.

When I entered the living room, I could see the light on in the kitchen, so I went that way.

"Pops?" I called out to him.

Silence.

"Aye, Pop...what you doing, nigga? Don't be eating up all the lunch meat."

I lived on sandwiches. If he was eating up all the lunch meat, I'd have to go out for breakfast in the morning.

"Pop—"

"It's not him. It's me," a familiar, but unclear female voice called out.

Without thinking twice, I reached under the countertop where I kept a piece. Even though my family had the code, I stayed ready for anything. I wasn't one of those paranoid niggas, however, I wasn't taking no chances.

"Who the fuck are you? Get the fuck out my fridge and show your face!"

Whoever this was didn't come to harm me. That was

for sure. I mean, she was in a nigga's fridge eating up the lunch meat. Still, I wasn't taking no chances. She could've been getting a snack before she tried to kill me. Again, I wasn't paranoid. Just cautious as fuck.

Slowly, she closed the fridge and backed away from it with her hands in the air. I backpedaled, my gun still aimed at her, to go turn on the kitchen light. Once it was on, I was shocked and a little confused to see her standing there with a sandwich in her hands.

"Fuck you doing here? How you get in?" I demanded to know.

Any evidence of me being on edge had fled my body. Although I should've been infuriated with Kori being in my kitchen, I was relieved. No lie, I had been thinking about shorty since we left the club. I even sent one up on her behalf.

"Okay, first, put the gun down. I come in peace. I just stopped by to check on you. That's all." she calmly stated.

"Okay, so how you get in?" I calmly questioned, gripping my gun at my side.

I knew who she was and knew she wouldn't hurt me. It was the thought of her having my access code and being in my fucking kitchen, eating up the lunch meat and shit that had me heated. Now that the lights were on, I noticed she had everything out to make a fat ass sandwich. She even had a big bag of unopened Nacho Cheese Doritos sitting there, ready to be opened.

"Put the gun down first," she calmly stated with her mouth full. Shorty was really eating a sandwich right now. Though she asked me to put the gun down, she didn't seem fazed by it.

"Nah, answer me before I shoot your ass," I threatened, completely serious.

"You're not going to shoot me." She smirked.

"You want to bet?" I stepped closer, turning my gun sideways.

"Please, Islah, if that were the case, you would've already done—"

Phuim!

"Keep talking that shit and calling me by my gov!"

"Are you fucking crazy?!" she shrieked, glancing behind her. The bullet missed her head by an inch.

"As hell. Especially when an unwanted guest is in my home. Now, you got five seconds to tell me how you know where I stay and who gave you the access code!"

I knew it had to be one of the fam. I put everything I had to my name on Rizz. Shit, it wasn't like I'd be losing anything. Her ass did it!

"So, you don't want me here?" She kept up this charade. I had to give it to shorty, though. She wasn't trying to snitch on her cousin, and I respected that. Her showing loyalty was an A+ in my book. However, I wasn't for this shit she was trying to get over on me.

Waltzing over to the elevator, I pressed the down button so she could get the hell on. The up button led to the roof, where there was an amazing view of downtown Chicago. You could also see some of the other sides of the city from there. I liked to go there whenever I needed to clear my head or didn't want to be found.

"Get the fuck out my crib, Kori!"

"Ohh, you did say you have that movie, huh? Let's watch it. I'll make us a sandwich and we can watch it together." She giggled like a maniac.

Man, this chick was off her shit. One minute, she was giving me the cold shoulder, kicking me out the crib. Next, she was showing up to my shit trying to play crazy. I wasn't sure if she was trying play 'get back' for what I did. I wasn't beat for this shit, though.

"You think I'm playing with your ass?" In a few strides, I was across the room and had ahold of her upper left arm.

She reached down and got a handful of my dick. My shit stiffened in her grasp. I was mad because my body had betrayed me. I didn't want to be hard for her right now. I wanted to be pissed and kick her little uglass out.

"Mmm, I told you it's mine." She licked her lips with a mischievous grin. My hand went to the side as I allowed her to slip her small hands into my pants. She gripped my dick and began to tug on it, trying to lead me in the direction of the kitchen.

In one swift movement, I scooped her up and carried her ass to the kitchen island. She was grinding her pussy against me and moaning with a handful of my dick. Pushing my ball shorts down in one swift motion, I gave her full access. My dick grew harder and longer as precum oozed from the tip. Kori licked her lips and bit her bottom lip.

That shit was sexy as fuck. This woman was doing some crazy shit to me. My body had never reacted the way it was doing with her. I was thinking and doing shit out of character for me. leaning over, I kissed shorty in the mouth. Now that definitely wasn't me. I didn't let no bitch kiss me in the mouth. Kori made me act differently though.

"Laaah…" she moaned deeply against my lips,

stroking me harder and faster. "I need to feel you inside me baby!"

Her wish was my command as I reached under her dress and snatched her panties off. Pulling her dress over her juicy ass, I eyeballed her pussy. Everything in me wanted a taste. I didn't believe in going down on woman unless she was my wife though. fighting the urge to plunge my tongue in her pussy, I used my dick as a replacement.

Slamming into her, I hugged her tight and close. Both me and Kori froze in place before our bodies shuttered. Her pussy was so hot and juicy, I had to count to ten in my head. I had to concentrate on something or else I'd be cumming fast and not slow.

"Fuck ma…" I spat under my breath. She started sliding back and forth on my swollen pole. We were on the island, yes. However, I had her a few inches off the island. Once I caught her rhythm, I took control, slowly slamming into her gushy walls.

Clawing my back, Kori started saying shit that made no sense at all. The only thing I could really make out was, "Mmm, fuckkk baby! Laaaaah, give it to me daddy!"

"How. You. Want. It?" I asked her with each deep stroke.

"Just. Like. That!" surprisingly, she kept up with me. I hadn't met a woman who could take all of me and keep up. They'd be screaming I was too much or too rough. Not Kori though. She was taking all of me and equally fucking me back.

God, where has this woman been all my life?

"Babyyyy! I'm about to cummmmm!" she moaned louder as I went deeper. Shorty fucked me up by squeezing her pussy muscles around me, sucking my earlobe at the same time. "Mmmm!"

Just as I felt her cumming, I pumped harder and faster. I had Kori bouncing off my dick, both her knees in the crooks of my elbows. Moving back some, I stared in her face. I fucking lost it at the way her mouth fell agape and her eyes rolled to the back of her head. I was now fucking Kori so good, her words got stuck in her throat. That alone had me ready to bust all in her walls.

Feeling her cum for the third time, I felt mines approaching vastly. Pulling out of Kori, I set her on top of the island and stroked my dick with one hand as I nutted in the other hand. The whole time she watched me, with her leg propped up and playing in her pussy.

Gotdamn she a freak! My mind was all over the place. I hadn't nutted so hard in my life. I completely drained and spent. All I needed now was a hot shower and my bed.

After we both caught our breaths, Kori hopped off the island, fixing her dress. "Where is your bathroom?"

I pointed to the nearest bathroom, before limping away to my own bathroom. Hopping in the shower, I washed our escapade off of me. By the time I got out the shower, I was hearing the elevator doors open and shut.

Ding!

Shaking my head, all I had the energy to do was shut the lights out and fall into bed. I got to change my access code.

CHAPTER 9

IYANNA "YANNA" BELL-CASIQUE

Three Weeks Later…

"**M**mm baby, shiiit! Just like that…" my husband groaned as I slowly rode all nine inches of his thickness.

Isiah Perez Casique was the best lover I'd ever encountered. To have him as my husband meant he was mine forever. I meant that shit — literally.

The minute we made things official, it'd been *us against the world*. Most people said that on some play-play shit. We were serious. We vowed before the vows. No matter what happened, we would stick together. It'd been eight years, and we were still hanging on. Though we'd been together for eight years, we'd been married for six. I was twenty and he was twenty-one when we were married. We were now twenty-six and twenty-seven. We met at eighteen and nineteen. I was attending the university and he was up there, posted on his baby blue old school Monte Carlo. I was minding my own business when he stepped to me.

I'm not going to lie. I judged the book by its cover on first approach. I tried not to. That's the way I was set up back then, though.

The thing about Isi was, he didn't look like the average thug back then. The nigga didn't have any visible tattoos. He didn't wear a grill. He didn't wear oversized jewelry or barely any jewelry, for that matter. His clothes weren't all baggy on him, and he spoke so proper. I mean, he still had the hood mentality or whatever, but he knew how to disguise it.

What made me know he was a thug was his demeanor. Well, that and the fact that his name buzzed all over campus. I'd hear females talking him up, saying he was the man, his whole family was bosses, they had the whole city on lock and shit like that — they would say even his mama was clutch. Not believing the hype, I stayed off the scene. I was in college for one sole purpose. I was a psychology major with a minor in social science. I planned on becoming a social worker. Chicago had a lot of shit swirling around with kids not having habitats. It pissed me off that they were on the streets. I wasn't too sure about social work at first because of all the shit that runs along with it. I just knew I wanted to work with the kids.

Anyway, Isi approached off bat. It was crazy to me because I didn't get why he would hang around the university. His family was supposedly "the shit." Why was he being average? Why wasn't he wearing some suit, sitting behind a big ass desk and ordering hits on people who were out to get him? Me being myself, that was one of the very first things I asked his ass. He thought it was funny, but sexy as fuck that I spoke my mind and wasn't shy. Shit, in Chicago? You couldn't be! You better know how to speak up, or else you might get beat the fuck up.

He told me I shouldn't believe everything I hear. Off bat, he was honest with me. He explained that his family did have certain parts of Chicago on lock, yes. However, his dad (and quite frankly, him as well) didn't trust a soul. These niggas were hand over fisting them damn selves.

He explained his pops' theory on 'never bite the hand that feeds you'. Basically, he didn't trust anyone but his family, who he knew wouldn't betray him. Their motto was, *us before anything*. Bottom line, you couldn't bite a hand that's been feeding you all your life. Pops made sure he instilled that into his kids.

Being with Isi was fun and scary, all in one. I never expected to fall in love the way I did with someone like him. He became my everything. Shit, I even joined the family business. Like Kendrick Lamar's songs says, *I got loyalty, royalty inside my DNA*. If my man was riding, I wanted to be by his side. He wasn't for it at first. I wasn't studying psychology for no reason. I put it to use on his ass, explained things from my perspective, told him how I could be an asset to the team. After he heard me out, we were literally joined at the hip. If I wasn't at school, I was with him doing whatever he needed me to do. If he wasn't in the streets, he was under me.

A lot of people wondered how we survived this long. Trust was the number one reason. I trusted him with my everything and vice versa. Anything I did, he knew and the same went for him. We couldn't take a shit without running it by each other first. That's how solid we were. Don't get me wrong. The hoes came flocking, but I trusted my husband enough not to do me wrong. The day he did…like Beyoncé said, *I pray I catch you whispering. I pray you catch me listening.* If not, that nigga might be dead before the dial tone.

"Shiiit! Get that shit, baby." He squeezed my hips and bounced me on his thick member all at once. The shit felt so good I was about cum.

"Babyyyy, I can't take it no more. I'm about to…shit!" I came all over his pelvis.

That didn't stop the show. He wasn't done with my ass. I was tapped out, but I couldn't pass out until he got his. That was another thing. If your man wasn't getting it enough at home, he might stray. Shit, some strayed anyway.

"Nah, fuck you think you doing? Daddy ain't finished yet," he growled as he flipped me onto my back. He didn't even have the audacity to move out of me. Just slammed my shit.

You'd think after eight years and counting, I'd be used to his girth. As much sex as we had, I should've been able to take it. That wasn't the case. Isi was all of nine inches, and thick! I was skinny and petite. My shit snapped back, and fast!

By the time he'd gotten his nut, I had cum another three times. After cleaning us both up and stripping the bed, he got behind me and wrapped me into his embrace. I didn't know I was crying until Isi wiped the corner of my eyes.

"It's okay, baby. Don't cry."

"I can't help it, babe. It just hurts so bad," I whimpered. No matter how hard I tried, I always cried after we had sex.

"It's going to happen, baby. Just give it time," he spoke with so much faith. "We'll have more time to—"

I cut him off. "Baby, but the doctor said—"

"Fuck what them doctors said, baby. I said it's going to be okay," he reassured with assertiveness. I hated to argue with him. My faith wasn't as big as his though.

"It's not okay, Isiah. I can't give you the one thing we both want. Sometimes, I feel like half a woman because of it. Or not a woman at all." I cried harder.

"Iyanna, dead this shit. I'm done talking about it," he snapped at me.

I lifted myself to get off him. I was in a straddled position. We usually fell asleep like this after a long sex session. He knew I was moving because I was in my feelings.

"Baby, I'm sorry for snapping. It's just, I hate when you get like this. You lose faith and start doubting and putting yourself down. I hate that shit, baby," he spoke his mind freely. One thing about the Casique family is they were all outspoken. They said the first thing that came to mind.

"I know Isiah, but—"

"No buts, babe. We're going to have a baby…soon. Fuck what those doctors say. You hear me?"

I didn't say anything else. It'd be no use and make no difference to Isi. He had it made up in his mind. He knew, in his heart, that we would have a baby one day. I, on the other hand, didn't believe we would. I believed the doctors. They made it clear that chances were slim to none that I'd conceive. I was diagnosed with a condition called endometriosis. It dealt with the endometrium, which is the lining of the womb. The doctors had explained this to me. Basically, the cells that normally grow in the endometrium were growing in other places outside my womb, so the baby wouldn't develop or the sperm would be ineffective. This is what the doctors said, though. Isi waved the shit off like it didn't mean a thing. Like I said, his faith was bigger than mine.

Laying against him, I studied the rise and fall of his chest. I listened to his breathing and light snores. I was wondering what he was dreaming about. These were the times I loved most. I would imagine us with a big family, like the one Perez and Kayla had. I never imagined pushing four out. If I could just get one, I'd be cool with it. more than that...*blessed*.

৩৩৩

I woke up to the smell of bacon hitting my nose. Mentally, I wasn't hungry, but the hunger pains churning at the pit of my stomach told me otherwise. After brushing my teeth and washing my face, I headed downstairs. I followed the voices coming from the kitchen. Liz was staying with us until Kayla and Perez came back. There was more than just her voice, though.

"Good morning, sleepy head," Isi greeted me first. He planted a few kisses on my mouth while squeezing my ass.

"Good morning, baby." I giggled. He kept massaging my booty. To be skinny, yet petite, I had a nice-sized derrière. Isi loved it. He used the term 'slim-thick'. I hated it because it was so average. "Stooop, nasty!"

"I wasn't nasty last night," he teased. My face grew warm. I knew it was probably red from embarrassment by now. Not only was Liz here, mama Casique, their grand-mother, was as well.

"Ugh, didn't y'all get enough of that last night? I mean, sheesh. I couldn't get no sleep, and now I can't even eat my breakfast. Damn!" Liz instigated with a smirk. I laughed because it was too early and she was already clowning.

"Baby, Mama is here. Stop that." I popped his hands away.

"Shit, she grown." He shrugged with no remorse evident in his tone.

Whap!

"Ahh, shit Grandma!" He rubbed the back of his head after she slapped him upside the head. I laughed because I knew it was coming. Mama Casique didn't play that disre-spectful shit. However, her responses to her grandkids' testing her were funny.

"Callate perro estupido!" she cursed in Spanish.

"Mama, how are you?" I hugged her. She squeezed me in a tight embrace.

"Yanna, mi amor. Come and sit. Eat." She pushed me into the chair next to Isi and set a plate of food in front of me. My stomach growled at the sight of all the food. On second thought, I guess I was a little hungry.

As I began to dig in, I could hear Lah and Rell go at it as they made their way into the kitchen. All you heard was a bunch of teeth smacking and mumbling. They usually did this when they were talking shit to one another.

"Aye, Frick and Frack! Come join us for breakfast and shut up," Mama shouted with her hands on her hips. They both came in and smiled at her. After they gave her a hug and some kisses, they came to the table.

"Well good morning, gorgeous." Rell bent down and gave me a kiss on the cheek. My mouth was too full of food to say anything back just yet.

"What's up sis? That morning after glow suits you." Lah kissed my cheek next.

"Watch it, nigga." Isi glared at him.

"I be playing. Shut yo uglass up." Lah waved him off with a laugh. I almost choked on my food. Being in this family, there was never a dull moment.

"Hey, y'all. Thank you for the compliments," I replied to them and stuck my tongue out at Isi. He gave me one of his 'don't get fucked up' stares.

After showing love to Liz and Isi, Rell and Lah sat in front of their respective plates. Mama Casique sat at the head of the table. Usually, Isi did because he was the man of this house. However, when she was here, he let her have her way.

She was Mama to us all. Really, she was Perez' mother. She, just like Liz, stayed with Perez and Kayla. Since those two were on vacation, Liz was over here. I guess Mama decided to come make breakfast at our house. She usually cooked for Kayla and Perez in the morning. Occasionally, we'd all end up over there to have breakfast.

"So..." Lah started to say. He now had all our attention, even as we were digging into our food. "Anybody heard from Kori?"

I was thrown off by the question. I was under the impression he didn't care for my boo. I knew the feeling was mutual with her. She made sure to let us know anytime we got together for drinks and food or a spa appointment. I really like Kori. She was a great addition to the family. I also thought her and Lah made a sexy couple, minus the craziness they both brought.

"Yeah, she just graduated Chicago State and started her new job." I told him.

Everyone except Lah, Kayla, and Perez were at her graduation. Ma and Pops were still on vacation, of course. Lah, I could guess a few reasons he didn't attend.

"Why?" I pressed on, biting into a fresh strawberry.

"She broke into my penthouse a few weeks back. I been wanting to see her little ass about that." he revealed with an evil glare.

My eyes and Liz's grew bigger. "How she find out where you stay? How did she even know the access code?" Liz beat me to the questions.

"Hmm, I have a good guess. I just thought I'd bring it up in case anyone wanted to volunteer information." Lah stared between Liz and me.

We both put our heads down and began eating again. His guess was as good as mine. I knew Kori was pretty upset at the way he treated her when they initially met. I didn't think she was stupid enough to show up at this man's house, though. Lah might've met his match in her. I didn't know a soul who'd be bold enough to play Lah's games with him.

"Who you suspect did it?" Rell asked. Isi was busy eating and, on his phone, doing whatever.

I noticed he was moving his thumb across the screen a lot. I could've looked over his shoulder. I didn't, though. He was always on his phone. Just like Pops, he was a workaholic. They were getting in position to resign their position in the streets. I was praying this would give Isi more free time. He deserved it for all the shit he caried on his bare shoulders. He couldn't stress enough how he was the oldest and had to keep things straight for his siblings.

Aside from the street dealings they owned a bunch of different businesses. Perez' goal was the same, in and out the streets. Take over the city of Chicago. I wouldn't be surprised if he was planning to run for Mayor one day.

"I know it was Rizz's ass who gave her my shit too." Lah sounded confident. Shit, he was probably right. After all, Kori is her cousin. She probably wanted Kori to get back at Lah.

Smack!

"Close your mouth. We don't want to see the STDs and *God knows what* swarming around in your mouth!" Mama squinted her eyes at Lah. She had popped him for talking with a mouthful of food.

"I ain't got no STDs, Mama. See…ahhh." He opened his mouth and stuck his tongue out. We all looked away. Liz and Isi started fake gagging.

Rell was too into his phone to care about his brother's table manners. Whatever he was doing had his face scrunched up. He was also becoming red in the face, placing his phone on the table, he joined the convo.

"I'll believe it when I see some results on paper. You fuck so many bitches you bound to catch something."

Smack!

Mama smacked Rell next. She'd just gotten up to retrieve the plates that were empty. "Watch your mouth! Get the hell off the phone. Tell Rizz while you on the phone with her, I hit her up and she hasn't hit me back."

"Oww Mama, damn. Why you always hitting a nigga?" Rell rubbed his arm.

"Because a *nigga* always on the damn phone. Don't be

talking to nobody but a Ken doll or my grandbaby-in-law. By the way, hit her up. Tell her to call me back." Now, we were all looking her upside the head. "Why y'all looking at me like that?"

"First, Mama, what we tell you about using slang? It's not for you. You're too old. Second, since when do you like Keyona?" Liz asked with a screw face.

Mama scowled. "First, little girl, I'm *your* elder. I can say what I want! Better put some respect in your tone. Second, who said I liked that damn Ken doll?!"

Hearing her say that, I almost choked on my juice. "Mama!"

"Yanna!" she yelped, mimicking me. "You know that heffa a man! Quit acting like we don't be talking about it at tea time!"

The whole table went up in laughter. Everyone was doubled over except Rell. He had a mean mug across his face. "Y'all just gon' disrespect my girl right in my face?"

The table got quiet for a minute, then we started up laughing again.

"Boy, hush up!" Mama spat. "Like you don't know you sleeping with a man! I got a question...which one of y'all is the top and which is bottom?"

Again, everybody except Rell was laughing.

"Mannn, Mama...whatever." He waved her off and went back to his phone.

"That better be my future grandbaby-in-law you're texting! Tell her to call me back!" Mama slapped the table. Rell looked up in confusion.

"Who are you talking about, Mama?" Rell seemed irritated when he asked.

Lah went into a coughing fit before blurting out, "Rizz!"

Rell pivoted his head in Lah's direction, cupping his ear in his hand. They were sitting directly across from each other. "Excuse me, brother. You gon' have to repeat yourself."

"And cover your damn mouth, boy. We don't want your herpes," Mama chimed in.

"Rell know what's up." Lah ignored Mama and winked at Rell.

Rell shrugged his shoulders in annoyance. It seemed like he'd been in a funk since being on his phone. Usually, he would laugh and joke with us. It never really mattered if the jokes were about *his soon to be wife*. This nigga was just in his feelings for whatever reason.

Just then, we heard the front door open and shoes click-clacking across the wooden floors. I knew it was Rizz off bat. She was the only other person besides the people in the room who had a key. My boo walked in looking stunning. Her cinnamon-chocolate skin was glowing almost as bright as the sun. She was wearing the hell out of this red strapless dress that hugged her curves.

Rizz knew she was too thick, with her fine self. She had thick thighs, wide hips, and just as much booty as me. She wasn't too big, nor too small in the waist area either. I loved her shape. It was beautiful and voluptuous.

"Heeyy, everybody!" She bounced into the kitchen with a Kool-Aid smile on her face. Her teeth were so white. They looked freshly polished. The twenty-inch bundles she rocked went perfect with her attitude and attire.

"Hey, boo!" I jumped up to give her a hug. "Ahh!"

Suddenly, I felt a sharp pain shoot up the side of my stomach and a little in my upper to middle back.

Isi caught me before my knees could even hit the floor. I noticed the chair he'd been sitting in was flipped over. His phone was sitting on the floor next to it. My baby was always right there to catch me before I fell and vice versa. "You okay, mama?"

"Yeah, I'm fine, baby. Is Yanna okay?" Mama answered in a concerned tone.

She knew he wasn't talking to her. She was just trying to be funny to not make a big deal out of things. She was good at taking the pressure off situations. She was also great at applying the pressure to situations.

"I'm talking to my wife, Grandma." Isi shot her a look. I knew he wasn't trying to come across rude. He was too focused on me to laugh at anything. Shit, even I laughed a little. "You good, baby?"

"I'm fine, babe. I don't know what that was about."

"I'm making you a doctor's appointment...right now." He picked me up in his arms. He had me cradled in his arms like I was a baby.

"Isiah, no. It's not that deep. I said I'm...aghhh." In the middle of me putting my foot down, it got chopped off. I had another pain shooting up my back and abdomen.

"See, shut the fuck up. I'm taking you now." He started paddling toward the door. Everybody was up and, on their toes,, ready to follow as well.

Isi eased me into the car in one swift motion. After buckling me in and shutting the door, he got in the car. I said a quick prayer that everything turned out okay, and that my husband was just tripping.

CHAPTER 10

RELL

"Ride with me," I whispered close to Rizz's ear. She wasn't paying my ass no mind as she texted away on her phone. I must've been loud enough for Liz to hear me.

"Nah, last time I rode with you, I got left at the club. Almost had to beat KEN-yona ass for talking out her Adam's Apple," she yapped. Palming my face, I blew out a breath. I swear my family had jokes.

"I wasn't talking to you, big head. Go get in the car with Lah's ass." I shooed her away. Right then, Lah walked up behind us, standing next to Liz.

"Why?" he challenged with a smirk.

Lah and I had pulled up at Isi's house at the same time. He wasted no time telling me he caught me and Rizz fucking last night. While he was clowning, he was also telling me I needed to be careful. Then, this nigga was asking me all these questions. Like, how long had we been fucking? Were we fucking as kids? Who all knew? When was the wedding? Shit like that.

"Yeah, why?" Liz joined her brother's antics. Sometimes, I swore Lah and Liz shared a placenta. He just came out before her while she delayed her arrival for two years.

"Y'all get out my business."

"Mhm! See, Lah! I told you they fucking." Liz cracked up. Little uglass was damn near choking with all the laughing she was doing.

"Hope you laugh out a lung, too." I playfully popped her upside the head.

I then turned to Rizz, who was all in her phone. She was just skinning and grinning all into the phone. I couldn't lie. The green-eyed monster was on my back. Who the fuck was she texting that had her about bustin' her fucking gums?

"Paris!" I called her gov. She flinched, her phone dropping to the ground. Silently, I prayed that bitch's screen was cracked. Fuck whoever she was texting.

"Ooouuu! First name basis and shit!" Liz was still standing there instigating and shit. I swear if I wasn't afraid to get into it with Pops or Isi, I'd slap her ass. "You hear that shit, Rell?"

"I heard it, ma. For real, let's go, though. Isi probably already at the hospital. Plus, *Israel* wants some alone time with *Paris*," Lah stated the last part in a teasing manner.

I mean, I cared about Yanna too. I just wanted Rizz to ride with me so we could talk on the way there. I needed to know where we stood, what was going on with us or something. It was crazy because we let one night of head turn into full-blown sex, and in Pops office at that! Then, while in the heat of the moment, we did it in the back seat of my car. Real life, I was confused and just wanted answers. Her asking me if I had feelings for her threw me off. Was she feeling some type of way about me too? I know females have sex with a guy and wonder those things. This was Rizz, though. We weren't supposed to cop feelings. Our relationship was supposed to be strictly platonic. We might've joked, but that's as far as it went.

"Ugh, Rell! Look what you made me do. This shit better not be cracked!" Rizz reached over and picked the phone up.

I couldn't resist the urge to peek at her ass in that dress. The fuck was she wearing that shit for anyway? The office was closed today. Even then, she never wore no shit like that to work. "Fuck that phone. Get in my car and let's go."

"No. Hell no! I'm rolling in my own shit."

"Rizz—" I had to stop myself and take a deep breath. I needed to talk to her. After this discussion, she could do what the fuck she pleased. I wouldn't interfere or nothing. "Get. The. Fuck. In. The. Car. now!"

She stood there with squinted eyes. I could tell she was thinking about it, like she was weighing out her options. Not saying a word, she snatched the car door open and got in. When I got in, she had her arms crossed and her bottom lip poked out like a big ass kid. I could've laughed my ass off, but I kept my composure.

"Okay, so talk, nigga," she said five minutes into the ride. Isi and Yanna didn't live too far from the hospital, so we'd be there in a few minutes.

"First, regulate your fucking tone when talking to me. You know I'm not some square ass nigga. I'll slap your ass, Rizz." She had the nerve to be yawning and checking her nails like she was bored. "Keep fucking playing with me, Rizz."

"Look, muthafucka. First, I'm not Keyona! I'll slap yo ass back. Second, what is it that you need to talk to me about? Shit, Rell! You been extra annoying to me all week."

"Who was you texting that had you skinning and grinning?" I let that question slip out my mouth. I wasn't going to say nothing. Then again, it'd eat at me if I didn't ask. I was taught that closed mouths didn't get fed.

I was supposed to ask about her feelings for me. We were going to talk about what was happening between us, if what we did was worth giving a try or not. Instead, I couldn't help myself. I had to ask her ass. I won't lie. I could be a jealous nigga. I was spoiled and liked what was mine to be exactly that —mines. No shame in saying the shit.

"I know damn good and well you didn't force me to get in this car for that. I just know you didn't waste my time like that." Rizz's head fell into her palms as she shook her head.

"So, what if I did? We best friends." I shrugged, not giving a fuck about her being irritated. I was irritated too. Keyona had been blowing my ass up all day. Rizz was acting like a nigga didn't matter to her. Shit.

"Exactly, Rell. We're *best friends*. Nothing more, nothing less. Why are you acting extra? You said you don't have feelings for me!" her voice shook a little when she yelled. Hearing the emotion behind her tone, I glanced at her. On the low, I was looking for tears or a sad face. That would tell me she felt some type of way about me too. She only had a mean mug on her face.

"*I swear, you give a nigga a little taste and they're breathing down your neck...*"

"I never said I didn't have feelings for you..." I confessed.

"So, what are you saying?" she kept her tone even and kept her eyes away from me. I hated when she did this.

It was like she was putting up a wall that wouldn't allow her to feel anything. The first time she'd done this to me was when I got with Keyona. It was around the time I was neglecting everyone to stay under Keyona. I can't lie, the shit hurt. It also irked, so much that I wanted to ring Rizz's fucking neck.

Pulling into the hospital, I found a parking spot and killed the engine. "Honestly, Rizz. I'm feeling some type of way about you. I'm trying to sort it out. Whether it's real feelings or it's because we had sex, I don't know. I know I don't like arguing or fighting with you."

"So, what do you want me to do, Rell?" she nonchalantly inquired. I took a deep breath in, and then left it out. This girl, I swear man. God, help me out, big homie. I'm going to send you an angel soon.

"I want you to be real, Rizz. Do you have feelings for me or what?"

"I don't know..." She shrugged and shook her head with an uncertain look on her face. "Even if I did and you did, it wouldn't matter. You're getting ready to marry Keyona and—"

"Mannn, I don't want to hear that shit! We not talking about her right now. This about us. I hate when you try and throw her in my face when shit gets too hot. Yes, I got a fiancée. She ain't got to be, though! What about you and this nigga you're with, huh?"

"You want to meet him?" she asked in a soft tone. "We could all go on a date. Like a double date or something."

Now, I was stuck. I wasn't expecting her to ask that. To be honest, I thought we'd just fight a little and end up having sex again, not her inviting me to chill in this nigga's face.

"Get out my car, Rizz."

Slightly turning in her seat, she stared at me sideways. "Are you—"

"Get out my car, Rizz!" I raised my voice an octave.

She popped her gums. "Ugh. Whatever, Israel. I'll see you inside." She got out the car, slamming the door and leaving me inside. I knew she'd be in her feelings for a while for the way I talked to her. At this moment, I didn't care.

I stayed in the car for a few more minutes. I was going back and forth with my feelings. Were they real, or were they just popping up because Rizz and I fucked? Shaking my head, I had to shake this shit, and fast. Rizz was supposed to be my best friend. I never wanted anything to come between that. It might've been too late, though.

The minute I entered the hospital, my mood changed from irritated to worry. I found the fam sitting in the waiting room with sad expressions. Liz, Mama, and Rizz all had tears in their eyes. Lah was blankly staring at the wall. Something told me this wasn't good.

"What's up, y'all? Is sis okay? Lah, what's up?" I went over and took a seat next to him. He shook his head. For a minute, I thought I saw tears in his eyes. My eyes weren't deceiving me when a single tear rolled down his face.

"She miscarried…" After saying that, he broke down.

Falling to my knees as he did, I held my baby brother in my arms. My shirt began to get wet from Lah's tears.

His face was buried in my chest. He hated crying in front of people. I did too, for that matter. My nigga was hurting.

We'd just lost one of ours, the first niece or nephew and grandchild to Ma and Pops. We were all feeling it. One thing was for sure. Isi was feeling it the most. I could only imagine how he was feeling or what he was doing back there.

CHAPTER 11

KEYONA "KEN-YONA" RUSSELL

I was just about to send Israel a text, like, *where you at???* but then he walked into the house. Usually when he walked in, he greeted me with a hug, kiss, a hello or something.

As of lately, this nigga was just walking in and not announcing himself. He wasn't being all lovey dovey like usual, nor was he asking me how my day was going anymore.

"Umm, hellooo to you too." I followed him to our bedroom. He didn't bother saying anything as he plopped on the bed with his head in his hands. His face was covered so I couldn't see his expression. Placing my hands on my hips, I shifted my weight from one leg to another. "I know you see me standing here."

"My bad, beautiful. What's up with you?" he looked up, shaking his head. If I wasn't mistaken, it looked as if he'd been crying. Pushing that to back of my mind, I got on his ass about *what was up* with me.

"I want to get married sooner," I demanded.

"What?" He looked me upside the head.

"I said...I want to get married sooner," I stated louder and with more aggression. Before he could say something, I started talking again.

"Baby, we shouldn't have to wait until July. I'm ready now. I mean, I got everything in place. We might as well do it now. This weekend. Please, Rell?" I probably sounded like a little ass kid begging their mammy for some candy right now. I didn't care, though. I wanted what I wanted. I was tired of pussy footing around with him on this marriage.

"No," he lowly confirmed.

I heard him but still asked. "What?"

"You heard me, Keyona. No. I'm not ready yet."

"You're not ready, why?" I stood with my hands on my hips. "Two years and you're not ready yet?"

"There's people who've been together for far longer that still ain't tied the knot, Keyona."

Turning my nose up, I said. "I don't give a fuck about those people. We're not them, Israel!"

"I know you better stop yelling in my fucking face! We ain't getting married until I'm ready, and that's what it's gon be. If we get married at all..."

"If? The fuck you mean, if? Nigga, you're marrying me! I ain't waste two years with you, put up with your ratchet ass family for you not to marry me!"

He had me highly fucked up right now. I knew it was his family who was in his head. They hadn't liked me since Rell, and I started going together. He was always telling me I needed to lighten up on them. *Be nice because they'll come around.* That was a bunch of bullshit and he knew it. Honestly, I didn't know why he was around them so fucking much. I mean, he knew they didn't like me. I'm the woman he's supposed to be in love with. The woman he's supposed to be getting married to. Shit like that hindered a good relationship. If it were up to me, he wouldn't be around them at all. It'd be me and him all the time, like it used to be — like it was supposed to be. I used to swear I lucked up when I got with Rell. I thought he was the perfect man for me. I mean, he was spending time, taking me places, we were making cute videos like 'couple goals', and the sex was on point!

One day, that shit all stopped. Well, it felt that way to me. It wasn't like we didn't still do some of those things we used to, we just didn't do them as often as when we first started. That was all due to him being around his family. I swear he let them make his decisions for him. Like now, the nigga has been pushing our wedding back going on six months now. We were supposed to be married at the beginning of the year. Look here, it's May and I'm ready NOW.

Rell wanted to get mad about me buying all those wedding dresses. If his ass just went ahead and married me, we wouldn't be having this conversation.

"Look baby, we gon' get married. Just not right now. Right now isn't a good time, though, baby." He tried kissing my shoulder and down my arm. I nudged him off.

"You don't love me like I love you," I lowly spoke, staring at the floor. I was trying to think of something saddening. This way, I could cry and get my way with him.

He smacked his lips. "Don't start that Beyoncé shit. Not tonight, baby. You know I love you like you love me. Would I still be here if I didn't?"

I shrugged. "I don't know anymore, Rell. You're not the same."

Finally, I got some tears to come. All I had to think about was how my life fell apart moving to Chicago. I'm originally born and raised in a small town right outside of Atlanta. My parents are wealthy realtors. I grew up in a two-parent home, went to the best schools, and was waited on hand and foot by nannies and maids.

I told Rell this bullshit story about them not caring, but it was all a front. Of course, they cared. If they found out the reason I'd come to Chicago, not graduated, and had been dating thugs, they'd lose their minds. This was another reason I wanted to get married to Rell so fast. I thought maybe if we were married, they would see how happy I was with him and let me live my life accordingly. They wouldn't care that I ended up pregnant and dropped out of college. They wouldn't think twice about it.

"Keyona, I'm not about to deal with this right now. I'm not feeling it."

"What's wrong with you anyway?" I finally showed some interest.

He shook his head at first. The next thing I knew, he was crying. His shoulders were shaking, face was red, and he was hiccupping. Slowly, I walked over to him. I stood in front of him, between his legs. I began to rub his shoulders. He'd never broken down on me like this before. It was new, so I didn't really know what to do.

"She lost the baby...my first—" He stopped mid-sentence to catch his breath and ended up breaking down harder. Pushing away from him first, I slapped his ass in the face.

"You got another bitch pregnant?!"

It was like I slapped the emotion out of him. He stood up and moved toward me with fire in his eyes. His eyes were red, brows furrowed. I looked down, and his hands were balled into fists. I wasn't afraid that he might hit me. He'd never done that before. I was more afraid of the look in his eyes or what was about to come out his mouth. I'd been messing with this man for two years. They say words don't mean nothing if there's no action. That shit was a whole lie. Rell made it a point to speak his mind. It didn't matter how the shit fell out his mouth. He didn't care if I cried or not. His theory was, *the truth hurts anyway*.

"R-Rell, I—" I began to stutter and stumbled over my words.

He grabbed me by the face. His fingers and thumbs were cusped under my chin. He was squeezing my cheeks so tight, I could feel them pressed against my teeth. My lips were poked out and wiggling like a fish. This was the closest he'd ever gotten to putting hands on me.

"Fuck you just say to me?!" he roared in my face.

He released me, pushing my head into the wall. It hurt on the low, not so bad that I felt it would leave a bruise, though. "I-I, umm...I just thought—"

"No, Keyona, you didn't think at all. You never do these days. If you do think, it's about your fucking self! You act like the world revolves around you. Guess what? It doesn't!"

"Rell, I'm s—"

"My sister had a fucking miscarriage. Instead of asking what's wrong with your man, you on my nuts about a fuck ass wedding!"

"Rell—" I tried to cut in again. He cut me off.

"I let that shit slide. I've been letting a lot of shit you do and say about my family slide because I love your ass. All that's about to change." He nodded his head with a distant look in his eyes. I can't lie, it was scaring me. He reminded me of a crazed man right now.

"Rell, what are you saying?" I asked innocently.

"The wedding is off as of right now. I need time to sort some shit out. In the meantime, I'll be at Isi's crib."

I followed him as he walked toward the closet. He grabbed the biggest suitcase and threw it on the bed. I watched as he scooped dirty clothes off the floor and threw them inside. He then took a few suits, some under-garments, and a couple pairs of shoes, then threw them in. Now, he was in the bathroom mumbling shit to himself.

Honestly, I could care less if he was mad, pissed, or *whatever*. I was more worried how many nights he was going to be away. Why did the nigga need such a big ass suitcase?

"You're going to Isi's...right. Then why you need that big ass suitcase, Rell? Huh?" I walked up on him, getting in his face.

He ignored me, acting like I wasn't standing there. I wanted to slap his ass so bad. Then again, I wasn't sure I was ready to suffer the consequences.

"Because I don't know when I'm going to be back. Or, if I'm coming back at all." He zipped the suitcase and bumped past me. He had the nerve to be crying. He wasn't bawling, but silent tears were rolling down his face. I should be the one crying.

I couldn't say anything because I didn't know what to say. I wanted to stop him. What was the use? He wouldn't listen to me anyway. He was dead set on going to 'Isi's crib'. I had a feeling he was lying. He probably was going to that bitch he called his *best friend's* house, Paris. From the jump, I didn't believe that shit. They were more than that. Either they were fucking on the low, or they used to fuck on the low. The proof was all in the way they acted toward one another. Rell even called himself getting upset whenever she decided to date someone. He'd mope around for days, talking shit about the person under his breath. Did he not know how that made me feel? Then, when I brought it up, he'd brush it off like I was the crazy one! It was all good because I had something for his ass. He wasn't the only one with a 'friend'.

The minute the front door closed, I grabbed my phone. Tapping my nails against the marble countertop, I glanced at them and noticed I needed a fill. *Hmm, I'll go to the shop after this.* I can pick out some more stuff for my wedding as well. I wasn't too worried about Rell's tantrum. I knew he'd be back. When he did come back, his ass was marrying me.

"Hello."

"Hey, what are you doing?" I cooed into the receiving end of the phone.

"I'm with my girl right now. What you need?" he asked like he was annoyed.

"I need you, baby. Let's meet up when you're done with her." I kept it sweet and sexy. I could've been rude and snappy. However, I needed him for more than just one thing.

Hearing his groan into the receiver, I didn't care. "Man, I wasn't tryna fuck with you tonight, Key. Unless you got something for me. I'm talking more than pussy. A nigga got bills too."

"I got you. Just meet me at our spot. I'll make it worth

your while." I smiled into the receiver. I really hoped he came. I was really going to make it worth his while if he did.

"Aight man, I'll see you later."

After ending the call, I went about my day.

CHAPTER 12
YANNA

To be pregnant and lose a child is one thing. To be pregnant and lose a child without knowing you were pregnant is another thing. I honestly didn't know how to look at this situation. It was bittersweet. Bitter because I lost the first niece or nephew and grandchild of the family. Sweet because I was told I couldn't get pregnant, yet I miscarried. Though my faith wasn't high, I was now on the optimistic side.

This whole time, my husband had been having all the faith. I didn't, though. I just knew those doctors were right. Now, I didn't know. I did know that I felt an emptiness inside of me. I wanted to fulfill it again by trying for another baby. I also wanted to get checked out again by a new doctor. I needed a second opinion on if I really did have endometriosis. If I did, how did I end up pregnant to begin with? These were the things that had been plaguing my mind for these three weeks.

Though the doctors were giving me answers, I wasn't sure I believed them anymore. Isi would always say that

God was a miracle worker. It wasn't that I didn't believe in him, or *God* for that matter. I was blinded by what I was told.

Knock, Knock,

"Baby?" Isi knocked on our room door, peeking his head inside.

I knew he was shaken up by the miscarriage because he was walking around like a stranger in his own home. For the last three weeks, he'd been knocking on doors before walking in to check on me. He was also asking me for permission to use stuff. It was a bit amusing.

At the same time, I was concerned about my husband. I knew him like the back of my hand. Isiah was partially blaming himself for this miscarriage. He probably thought it was because of us having sex so wildly that night before, or him not letting up after my first climax. As his wife, it was my duty to assure him that none of this was his fault.

"Come on, papi." I patted the spot next to me on the bed.

I'd been resting in the bed since coming home. Ironically, I had to wait the same amount of time to have sex as if I had a baby. We were halfway through our six weeks. I was excited because I wanted to try for another baby ASAP.

"What are you doing?" he asked.

"The same thing I've been doing for the last three weeks," I replied with a smirk.

He rolled his eyes like he was that annoyed. I giggled a little. It still kind of hurt to laugh too hard. "Well, your real nigga home now. Those other niggas ain't real."

"Okay, hater. You got my attention," I smiled at him.

Since I'd been laid up, I decided to catch up on some

reading. I loved all types of genres. However, urban fiction was my favorite. Recently, I'd just finished *You Ain't Gotta Be Perfect* by Bianca. All I can say is get the book! Currency is B A E! Right now, I was catching up with part two of *I'd Rather Be Ya Hitta* by Porschea Jade. Babyyyy, Hamin and Ace can be my side niggas any day!

Isi laid his head in my lap. He had his big and muscular arms wrapped gently around my waist. I hummed as I stroked his fresh fade. I allowed my fingers to travel down as I combed through his full beard. Everything about this man, I loved. From his full Hebrew beard to his crème brûlée skin tone. As time went on, he got a few tats. They were all in places he could hide them, though. Staring down into his face, my eyes landed on his perfect pink lips. They were small, but full enough to give juicy kisses. Finally, I focused on his deep brown bedroom eyes. Distantly, he stared off into space.

"You know it's not your fault, right?" I spoke just above a whisper. I was now staring off into space. I was imagining what it would've been like to carry out a full pregnancy.

He sighed and kissed the palm of my hand and fingers. "Tell that to my heart, ma."

Gently, I nudged his shoulder and he turned over for me. He was now laying on his back, his head still in my lap and his eyes fixated on mine. I leaned down, kissed his lips, and then laid my head on his shoulder. I was trying to get as close to his chest as I could.

"You know it's not your fault, right?"

He began to laugh, causing my head to be jostled around on his chest. I sat up and stared down into his dark brown orbs. He had tears lining the corners of his eyes and some stuck in his eyelashes.

"I can't help but think it's my fault, baby. I mean, we were going kind of hard that night." As he spoke, the tears in the corners of his eyes slid down the sides of his face. I caught them before they could touch our blue and white bedspread.

"You heard the doctors, babe. It had nothing to do with sexual activity. Neither of us did anything wrong. It happens to women every day." I continued to wipe the tears forming and threatening to leave his eyes. "We're going to get through this together, okay?"

He nodded, but I wasn't convinced he believed me. "Where's all that faith you try and force on me?"

He shrugged his shoulders and sighed.

"Well, I'm going to need for you to channel that shit and put your best foot forward. We're not letting this get us down. It hurts me too, but baby, we're going to be alright."

"Okay, Ms. Lamar." He cracked a smile. Him smiling caused me to smile too. Anytime Isiah smiled at me, my heart skipped several beats. I couldn't help it. I loved this man 'til the death of me. Even then, I'd love him immortally.

"We gon be alright. We gon be alright. We gon be alright!" I chanted while doing the milly rock. Isi cracked up until he was red in the face. I could still see the tears, but knew they weren't all that sad anymore.

"Man, I swear, I married my best friend."

"I love you, baby." I planted kisses all over his face.

He kissed the back of my hand and my palm. "I love you more."

We were wrapped up in a make-out session when someone knocked on the door. Recently, we had both Liz and Rell staying with us. Pops and Kayla were due back last week but decided to stay a little while longer. I wasn't mad at them because Pops needed the time off. That man would work himself to death if Kayla let him, which she didn't.

Rell was here because he was into it with the Ken doll. It was crazy because she was in the wrong, yet Rell was here blaming himself. I hated when he did that. Keyona wasn't making it no better because she'd been blowing his phone up about pointless shit, stressing my bro out every chance she got. Then, Rizz wasn't speaking to him. I didn't get into that. Whatever it was would come to light eventually.

"Come in," we answered in unison.

"Aww," Liz and Lah walked in.

These clowns were wearing onesies. Liz's was fire truck red. She had a brown teddy bear in her hand. Lah's was Blue's Clues. He was holding a black flask and his onesie was unzipped, showing his bare chest. This nigga here. I couldn't stop laughing because they looked like they were big ass kids.

"What y'all lil' niggas want?" Isi laughed at his siblings.

"We're having a sleepover. We're ordering pizza, Netflix & chill, and might even play some board games," Lah started to explain. "That is, if you're up for it, sis."

"We just wanted to take your mind off the...you know..." Liz solemnly uttered. She hung her head and hugged her bear.

"Aww, I have the sweetest little brother and sister." I

moved out of the bed. I was still in a little pain. It wasn't enough to keep me bound to a bed, though. "Okay, how about y'all go move the furniture in the family room. Get the tents and set them up."

"Ayye! We're going to make s'mores and tell scary stories too." Liz rubbed her teddy bear's paws together with a devious grin on her face. Turning on her heels, she pulled her phone out the pocket of her onesie.

"Who you about to call?" Isi called out. It was too late. She was already out the room. "And you." He directed to Lah, who was taking a sip from his flask. "What are you drinking on?"

"Apple juice," Lah smirked. Laughing a little, I shook my head. We both knew he was lying. "I'm about to go set up these tents."

After he left, Isi and I were left in the room. He came behind me and wrapped his arms around my waist. "You sure you up for this, mama?"

Nodding my head, I answered. "Yeah, baby. It'll be good to around the fam. Especially with the fourth coming up. We can talk plans. I was thinking we could spend it at the lake house. It'll be fun to be away with everyone there."

"Okay, baby. That sounds cool to me. Let me get your onesie." He walked into our closet.

"You mean *our* onesies," I corrected, following him into the closet.

"That shit gay, baby. I ain't wearing that shit. You might as well throw me in a romper." He shook his head with distaste written all over his face.

"Ohh! That might look cute on you, babe!" I cheered, clapping my hands.

"*That might look cute on —* don't get fucked up, babe." I laughed at how he started off mimicking me, then stopped to finish the sentence.

"Lord baby, I just be playinggg." I giggled.

"You promise you won't laugh when I come out this closet?" He sounded ashamed. I giggled a little, not knowing what he was about to do.

"I promise," I replied, hardly containing the grin that threatened to turn into laughter.

"Okay, here I go…" He came out in the onesie I'd gotten him as a joke for Christmas. I wanted him to put it on then. He wouldn't do it because he claimed he was too big and would look 'gay'.

"Aww!" My eyes lit up. "Look at you!"

"I'm only doing this, this one time—for you!" he made it clear.

"Aww, I love you so much. You make me so happy, babe." Slowly, I walked over to him. The closer I got, the more I noticed his onesie was a bit tight. "Baby?"

"Huh?"

"You sure you got on the right one?"

He began to turn in circles, trying to read the tag. I had to laugh because he reminded me of a dog chasing its tail. "Awl damn! I got on yours!"

Standing there, I shook my head. "Well, no wonder you look like Steve Urkel in it. Can your nut sack even breathe?" I felt him up.

He moved back. "Watch it now. Don't start something you not ready for."

"Mhm, I got you in three weeks." I stuck my tongue out at him. He moved in close to me. Bending his 6'2 frame down, he met with my 5'7. We shared a kiss so deep, I felt that shit in my toes. I had to wiggle them just a little bit.

Once we were dressed in our *rightful* onesies, we went to join everyone else.

⁂

Two hours later, Rell and Rizz joined the gathering. They too had their pajamas on. We were sitting in a circle with several boxes of pizza in the middle us. Everyone was quiet, in our own thoughts. You could tell these past weeks had been a little stressful on us all. It was only right that we had a moment of silence.

Ding, Dong…

We all got up at the sound of the doorbell. Everyone that mattered was here, other than Mama, Perez, and Kayla, that is.

"I'll get it," Liz volunteered, beating us to the door. "Hey, lil' mama! Ooouuu, you're looking fione."

"Oh Lord, you know you need to quit." A feminine voice giggled. I didn't know who it was until Liz came walking back in with her arm draped around her shoulders.

"*Koriiii!*" Rizz and I both ran to her. We all embraced like long lost best friends.

"Hey, babes!" she hugged us back. "How are you doing, mama?"

"I'm good, boo. Thanks for asking." I hugged and kissed her cheek.

Next, Isi and Rell came over to greet her. It was all love. After them, it was Lah. When they laid eyes on each other, the room grew silent.

We were watching the tension and attraction rising off their bodies. Neither were smiling. They both held grimaces. If I didn't know any better, I'd think they were scorned exes.

"Stalker," Kori held her hand out to shake his. Everybody else got hugs.

Lah stared down at her hand like it had shit on it. "Trespasser." He then walked off into another direction.

I had to say a quick prayer. I could see the direction this night was going to go in. *Lord, help us all.*

CHAPTER 13
LAH

Why? Why is it that I always get set up? Man, Liz got jokes for days. Once again, I was stuck in a room with Kori's fine ass. Let us just pray she don't follow me home again.

"Why are you acting like you not happy to see your future wife and baby mother?" Liz came into the kitchen, pulling me from my thoughts. I was standing by the sink with the water running and looking out the kitchen window.

Since I was a kid, the sound of water running calmed me down. Right now, I needed it most. Being around Kori brought out emotions I wanted to keep harbored. It'd been three weeks since our last encounter.

I ain't thought about her, and I'm sure the feeling was mutual. I heard she'd graduated, though. I was happy for her and everything. I wanted to send some flowers or something. Instead of just doing it, I let my pride get in the way.

"I knew your ass did this. Why you invite her?" I

turned and got in Liz's face. She was smirking like shit was funny.

I wanted to slap the smirk right off her face. I would've if I wasn't scared of the consequences. I was never afraid to say that my big brothers and Pops scared the fuck out of me. I mean, they were big compared to me. I had weight and height on me. However, they had more.

"She's family. She should be here." She shrugged like she didn't do anything wrong.

I squinted my eyes at her little ass. She was completely taking this as a joke. That, alone, was pissing me off. Why couldn't anybody understand that I didn't want this girl around me? She made me feel some type of way I'd never felt before. The craziest thing about her was, she didn't seem to take me seriously. She just acted like I wasn't there or some shit. I had to snatch her ass up just to make her notice me. That little stunt she pulled popping up at my house took the cake. I still hadn't gotten in Rizz's ass for it, as if I could. She was busy doing Lord knew what with Lord knew who. She was acting all anti and shit with the fam. Tonight was the first time I'd seen her since the miscarriage.

"Bullshit. That's Rizz's people. She ain't no kin to us." I shook my head and shut the water off. At this point, it wasn't doing anything but annoying me.

"That's where you're wrong. She's Uncle Pierre's niece. You know, *Aunt Viv's* daughter?" Liz still had that goofy ass smirk on her face. The people she listed weren't family by blood, but loyalty.

Uncle Pierre was Rizz's dad, my dad's deceased right-hand man. Aunt Vivian was Uncle Pierre's little sister. I'd only met her a few times. She was cool, though. I never put two and two together. Aunt Viv lived out in Portland. The last time I'd seen or spoken to her was at Uncle Pierre's funeral.

That was some sad shit too. Unc got capped out by some hating ass nigga. It was ironic because they killed each other. Unc was like fuck that. If I'm going out, yo ass is too. Man, I missed his ass. His birthday was coming up. That day was going to be a toughie for us all.

Liz had just told me Kori was Aunt Viv's daughter. Still, I had to ask. "How you know?"

"I was at the mansion earlier and ran across a pic of Ma, Pops, Uncle P and Auntie Viv. They looked young as fuck. You know it had to be hella ago. Like the fifties." She cracked up joking. I laughed at her dumb ass. She knew damn well Pops and Ma weren't born in the fifties.

"Anyways, I kept looking at Aunt Viv. Kori look dead on her when she was a teen. Rizz resembles her a lot too. Before putting two and two together, I hit Pops up. He confirmed my suspicions," she noted.

My eyes bucked at the mention of Pops. "Yo, you called Pops?! He doesn't know what happened to sis, does he?"

We all agreed to wait for him and Ma to get back to tell them. We didn't want to ruin their vacation. If they found out, they'd be on the first thing smoking. They were supposed to be back a week ago. Instead, they decided to stay another week.

Liz's face flushed red. That told me all I needed to know. She'd told him everything. Liz, just like my brothers and myself, couldn't keep shit from our pops, no matter how hard we tried. We would all agree and make a pact not to tell, but one of us — if not all — would end up babbling.

"You snitch b—"

Just then, I felt my feet lift two inches off the floor as my air supply was cut off. "Say it. Snitch what? *B—can I buy a vowel?*"

I was struggling to breathe as I kicked my legs around. Isi had my ass hung up by the neck. I felt like I was real life about to die. The next thing I heard was Liz laughing.

"Isi put him down. We were playing around. You know he wouldn't call me no bitch."

Isi released me. "You know I don't play that shit."

I would've responded, but I was busy trying to regain my air supply.

"Damn. You aight, nigga?" Rell walked into the kitchen next. He too had a smirk on his face. See, these niggas got jokes.

"Fuck y'all," finally, I caught my breath and spat. "I'm telling Daddy when he gets here too."

"*Snitch bitch!*" they all shouted. We were all laughing now.

"Who called Pops?" Rell asked in an annoyed tone.

Liz began to walk out the kitchen with her head in her phone. I grabbed her and pulled her back. "Don't run now."

"I didn't mean to! I was only asking about some family related shit." She hid her face.

"Family related shit?" Isi and Rell asked in unison. I already knew, so I stood back and chilled while she told off on herself.

"I just had a few questions about Aunt Viv. He gave me my answers, then started questioning me down about what was happening at home. Y'all know I couldn't lie to him."

"*True*," we all had to agree. Nothing got past Pops. He was like a human lie detector. The one time you tried to lie and, in his face,, be prepared to get beat the fuck up.

"What exactly is *everything* though?" Rell pressed on.

"Umm…" She stalled with a red face. Bingo! She told him more than what was happening with Yanna and Isi. If she told him what I think she did, Pops was sure to be on a plane back to the States.

"Spit that shit out, Eliza!" Rell barked.

"I told him about people inquiring about our name…" She cowered into the corner where the sink was. She no longer had a smirk. She more so looked like she wanted to cry. This was what always got to me about Liz. I hated to see her down. She was such an enthusiastic and playful person.

"What?!" both Isi and Rell shouted.

Isi looked angry, like he was ready to punch some-thing. Rell, on the other hand, looked confused. This nigga was out of the loop. I stood back and didn't say anything. I knew just as much as Liz. I hadn't had time to go and investigate because I was busy trying to find another marketing consultant. That's when realization set in.

Pops was coming back!

I hadn't met with Kori like he ordered. Nobody, for that matter. Man, this nigga was about to be HOT! He was going to go on and on about how irresponsible his kids were.

"I wanted to tell him that shit in person!" Isi slammed his big fist into the marble counter. I wondered if it hurt. His hand was red. He hadn't grimaced or made any noise about it, so I didn't know, unless he was just good at taking the pain.

"Who inquiring about our name?!" Rell yelled, still out of the loop. This nigga looked between a mixture of mad that no one was speaking up and worried. Therefore, he was confused.

"Nobody." Isi lowered his voice.

"I found him…" Liz lowly spoke. We all turned to look at her.

"Huh?"

"I mean…I didn't find, find him. I just have a clue on *where* to find him. I did some research and—"

"You been eavesdropping, haven't you?!" Isi didn't give her a chance to explain. Smacking my gums, I was getting irritated as fuck. If he would shut up, we might be able to get at the nigga. Pops wouldn't have to get involved and we'd be good.

"Man, shut up! Let her talk, shit!" I defended her. I wanted to know where and who the nigga was. I was eager as to why he was wondering about our family. If he was a threat, the nigga would be dead — on site. Isi shut up but mean mugged the fuck out of me. I didn't care. I just wanted to hear my sister out.

"As I said, I don't have an exact name for him. I know it's a guy because of the info I got. I'm still getting shit together. Give me a week, two tops and I'll have something for you." Liz was all in. The look of seriousness on her face told me she was down for whatever, or at least she wanted to be down.

Like a ticker on a clock, I could see the wheels in Isi and Rell's heads moving. Isi's face spoke, *Hell no. No, fuck no!* Rell's said, *I want to give her a chance, but ehh.* Now me, I was all for sis doing this. If she had the juice and no one else did, then why not? Of course, somebody would have to be with her. I'd volunteer if we found this nigga.

"I say yes," I spoke up first. Isi and Rell looked at me like I had just grown another head in front of them. I didn't care. "If sis can help, let her. The fuck? You niggas can do better? I know I damn sure ain't got the smarts to be hacking shit and doing that P.I. shit she knows. My ass been shot the first nigga I assume, on Mama."

Cluck!

"Ah, shit, gotdamn—"

"Don't be lying on me, pendejo!" I turned around, and Mama was standing there. Looking on the floor, I noticed her phone lying next to my foot. This old ass lady just threw her damn iPhone at the back of my head.

"Damn, Mama. A nigga just saying." I rubbed the back of my head.

"Don't just be saying, *on mama*. With ya fake gang-banging ass!" she emphasized. "My phone better not be broken neither! Big headed little boy!"

Man, my granny was crazy as hell! All I could do was laugh and continue to rub the back of my head. Yanna had just come in and whisked Isi away. Good, because that nigga was stupid mad. All Liz was trying to do was help her big brothers out.

"This meeting ain't over," Rell pointed toward us before heading back to the living room. Liz was still in the corner near the sink. From the look on her face, I could tell she was still on edge from Isi yelling at her. This nigga never yelled at her.

"You cool, sis?"

"Yeah. Thanks for having me." She nodded her head with a half-smile.

"You know I got you, mama." I pulled her into a hug. "Don't worry about bro. He just concerned about you. We don't want nothing to happen to you, ya know?"

"I feel you." She pulled away, nodding her head. "I'm going to go and get some stuff for the s'mores."

"You want me to go too?"

"Nah, I think I got it. Aye, did you ever try and hire a new marketing consultant?"

Her bringing it up reminded me of what I still needed to do. Just thinking about it made my head hurt. "Nah, I will, though. Pops is going to be on my ass if I haven't hired somebody by the time he gets back."

Just then, Kori came in. She was all in her phone with an ugly ass grin on her face. Real shit, it wasn't ugly. I was just irritated that she was here and probably entertaining some nigga. I didn't know why I cared so much, but I did. I wanted to slap that damn phone out her hand and walk away like a boss.

"Aye, Kori, you want to go to the store with me?" Liz asked her.

She looked up from her phone for a split second. She was still smiling like no tomorrow. Who was I kidding? This girl was gorgeous. Her pajamas were on point too. She was giving off TLC vibes when they did the video with pajamas. She even had on some cute little three-inch kitten heels. Damn, the shit I was thinking... having her pinned against the sink with them shits in the air as I fucked her brains out.

"Yeah, boo, let me get my jacket out the room Yanna took it to."

"Okay, mama. I'll be out in the car." Liz walked out.

Kori began to walk out too. I followed her until we got to the room her coat was in.

"What do you want, stalker?" She hadn't even looked behind her. She just knew I was following that ass.

"You, trespasser." I grabbed her around the waist and was holding her. I was trying to get a peek of who she might be texting.

"Boy, move…stop, Lah!" She pushed me off her.

"Yo, who are you texting?" I finally asked, taking a step back. "Why are you calling me *Lah* all of a sudden? You treating me like I'm some common nigga and shit."

"First of all, don't worry about who I'm texting. Second, you been wanting me to call your ass *Lah* since we met. I'm not about to play these games with you. Move out my way, *Lah*."

We stood there in a stare down. I was getting lost in her eyes. Biting my bottom lip, I waited for her to respond. Usually when I bit my bottom lip, the panties dropped. Kori stood her ground, though.

"I'm not going to tell you again. Move out of my way, *Lah*. I'm not feeling you like that." she cut her eyes at me.

"You're lying, but I'll let you have that." I backed up to let her by.

Kori could front all she wanted. She wanted the kid. She said it herself. My dick was hers. If shorty played her cards right, she could have it tonight.

CHAPTER 14
KORI

"So, you know you sharing a tent with Lah, right?" Liz asked, breaking the silence in the car.

She'd caught me completely off-guard. I was on my phone, going over what I'd be doing for Kassidy Kyle in the coming week. I was so happy with the new job I took.

"Umm, who? You mean Paris and Yanna?" I turned in my seat to glance at them sitting in the back.

Paris was cheesing all in her phone. Yanna was staring blankly out the window. I could guess a million things Paris was doing. Yanna, on the other hand, I was concerned about.

Hearing about her miscarriage hurt me to the core. The fact that she didn't know was like pulling the plug. I damn near flatlined. When Liz texted and told me what she and Lah were doing to comfort Yanna, I wanted to be a part of it. I didn't care that I had a lot to do in the morning. I could leave and go from their house.

"No, you K O R I," Liz spelled my name out.

I rolled my eyes hard and crossed my arms over my chest. "I'm glad you know how to spell. Furthermore—"

"*Furthermore*? The fuck? Girl, if you don't take yo bad and bougie ass on somewhere." Liz cut me off to make fun of my word choice. This bish was cackling hard enough to choke on her esophagus.

"Yes, bish. *Furthermore*, I'm not sleeping anywhere near your brother. If you only invited me to try and make us hook up—"

Again, she cut me off. "Ahh, yada-yada, yeah, yeah, yeah. Ain't nobody trying to hook y'all up. Besides, he told us what you did." She snickered.

I guess Yanna had gotten in tune with the conversation now. "Kori, please tell me that nigga was lying. You didn't really show up to his doorstep, did you?"

Liz was laughing hysterically. I swear she irked every nerve in my soul. This girl found everything to laugh about. "Sis! *Showed up on his doorstep*? Lah said Kori *walked in*. This bish trespassed!"

"Yeah, yeah. Kori, did you?" Yanna sounded anxious. I was too embarrassed to look at her. I'm sure my face was flushed.

"Yes, I did. I was only there to check on him. Then, I got ahead of myself and thought I could play games with him," I revealed.

"Girl, that nigga don't play games. You better be glad y'all were acquainted. Better yet, you family. He would've killed yo ass!" Liz said on a serious note. "Lah ain't got no good sense when it comes to shit like that, trust."

"Mhm," Yanna cosigned.

I blew out an annoyed sigh. "So, it's okay for him to show up to my doorstep unannounced, but I can't do it to him?" I was pouting in my seat. How were they going to get on me? Lah was in the wrong too.

"He didn't trespass, though, baby girl. You let him in. Did you not?" I knew Liz was only defending her brother, as she should. If I had brothers, I'd go hard for them as well. The closest thing I had to a sibling was Paris. Lord knows I'd go to war for her.

"I guess…" I rolled my eyes.

"Even if he did do it to you, you can't do it to him," Yanna added. I turned and looked her in the eyes. She did a Kanye shrug. "That's just the way the Casique men work. You can't do to them what they do to you."

"So, you're telling me I have to just accept that bull-shit?!" I shrieked.

"Damn, white girl. Get out my ear." Liz looked to me and back to the road, rubbing her ear.

Moving close to the ear she was rubbing, I screamed, "Fuck you, L I Z!"

She swerved a little. That got Paris' attention. "Jesus, Liz! Don't be doing no reckless shit with me in the car!"

Yanna, Liz, and I all looked back and forth between one another. We silently did this until we burst out laughing. Paris shook her head with a smirk. "I hate y'all."

"*We love you too!*" we retorted in unison, still laughing.

"Who got you cheesing back here?" Yanna asked with amusement in her tone.

Liz coughed out. "*Rell!*"

I laughed because she was trying to be slick. Next, Paris coughed out. "You a damn lie!"

"Bullshit!" Liz coughed out, and then used clearing her throat as a decoy.

"You wish!" Paris followed suit.

"I." *cough* "Do." *cough* "So why you." *cough, cough* "Playing?!" *cough*

Paris cleared her throat. "He." *cough* "Playing!" *cough, cough*

"Aha! So, you do want him!" Liz called her out. Me and Yanna were dying laughing. I couldn't recall when the last time I laughed so hard.

In Portland, I didn't have many friends. They were more like associates. The one friend I did have growing up passed when we were in eighth grade. She had just turned fifteen and had an asthma attack. After her, I didn't consider anyone else a friend. It wasn't until my mama started letting me go and visit my uncle and cousin in Chicago that I found a new friend. Well, I found a friend in Paris.

Even back then, she'd tell me about this boy named Rell. I'd never met him or his siblings because they were always out of town when I came there. It was usually the summer, so they'd be on vacation somewhere. Now that we were older, I was finally able to put names and faces together.

Meeting this damn family was something else, especially Islah's dumb ass. Ugh, that man knew he was fine as fuck. The way he was licking them lips earlier had me creaming in my pajama bottoms. I didn't wear any panties so if I had an orgasm, it'd surely tell off on my ass.

"I do not want him. It's the other way around," Paris stated in a matter-of-fact tone. I had to turn and glance at her. She was side smirking. We made eye contact, and I began to cheese.

"You nasty bish. What y'all do?"

Her eyes got big. "What you mean?"

Whenever her eyes got big and she had to repeat the question, she was lying her ass off. "You know what I mean. You and Rell did something, didn't y'all?"

"Spill the tea, bish!" Liz was finally pulling into Walmart. Isi and Yanna lived almost an hour away from it, so it took us some time to get here.

"Gon' now! Ain't nothing happened!" She got loud.

It was Yanna's turn to speak. "You lying! Everybody that knows you knows that you get hella loud when you're lying. Tell us. We're your girls."

Liz and I moved our heads closer to hear better. All you could hear was our heavy breathing as she twiddled her fingers. She was looking down at her lap at first. Looking up, she made eye contact with us all. "If I tell y'all, y'all have to promise not to say A N Y T H I N G!"

We all nodded our heads, waiting for her to tell us. "Okay, so...NOTHING HAPPENED! BYE BIHS!"

Before Liz, Yanna, and I realized it, she jumped out the car and took off running toward Walmart's entrance. All three of us sat there staring amongst ourselves. Paris could say what she wanted. However, I knew something was going on with her and her 'best friend'.

It was obvious in the way they were acting toward one another. To me, it seemed like Rell was angry with her. Paris was cool as a cucumber. He was breathing down her neck, trying to get all in her business. He'd get mad when she walked away without giving him a response. His ass was tripping — HARD! If I wasn't mistaken, this nigga had a *whole* fiancée. That wasn't none of my business, though. Paris just better know what she was getting herself into with him.

Staring at the clock, it was going on midnight. Unlike Liz said, I wasn't in a tent with Islah. I ended up in there with her. Right now, I was in the kitchen with the water slowly running. I didn't want to turn it on full blast in case I might wake someone. The only light I had on was the stove's light. Leaning against the countertop, I was deep in my thoughts.

I was thinking about my ma. I had sent her a train ticket to Chicago from Portland. She refused to fly. It wasn't that she was afraid. She just liked scenery and extra thinking time. She'd have three days to do so. While I was nervous to see her, I was excited too. I hadn't seen her since Christmas. That was exactly five months ago.

"What are you doing up, trespasser?" Lah walked into the kitchen, scaring me.

"Nothing. I couldn't sleep."

He lightly scoffed. "Thought you'd be stealing lunch meat."

Giggling and shaking my head, I replied. "Fuck you, Lah."

He would choose now to be petty and bring that shit up. I swear, I wouldn't attempt to ever make this man a sandwich again. He could've been starving with no limbs. I didn't care. Don't think, for a second, I forgot about him pulling that gun out on me. While it was sexy in a weird way, it scared me. His sisters weren't lying when they told me what they did. Shit, I'd witnessed it firsthand.

"We did that already, ma. Just say the word and I'll have your sexy ass hemmed up on the sink with the water running and them little heels you were wearing. Where they at?" He stepped into my personal space and looked down at my feet. The *sandals* I'd worn to go with my pajamas were hurting my feet inside Walmart. I couldn't wait to take them off and switch into some fuzzy non-slip socks.

"I took them off. I meant what I said, Lah. I'm not feeling you. Go away." I attempted to push him away. He wasn't budging. I swear, it was like this man lived to irritate me.

My mama used to tell me, people only do what you allow. Was I allowing him to irritate me? Why was it so hard for me to ignore this nigga? I hadn't known him but a few weeks and he got under my skin already.

"You're feeling me," he confidently stated. I rolled my eyes because he was so cocky. It was one thing to just be sure of yourself. He was cocky and it was annoying as hell, he just knew I wanted his ugly-fine ass. "I'll chill, though. It's not good to mix business and pleasure anyway."

"B-business?" I stuttered out. See, now I knew he'd lost all the sense God had given him- if any. The last I checked, he fired me before he hired me.

"Yeah, I'm hiring you on my team. You'll be at my place on Wednesday, 9AM sharp."

"Who in the hell do you think you are?" I stepped into his personal space. He caressed my upper arms and shoulders.

"You already know the answer to that. Need I remind you?" He lifted me up to where I had no choice but to straddle his waist so I wouldn't fall. I was about to protest when he sat me on the sink. "Look at your little ass. Scared but intrigued."

"Boy, please. Ain't nobody scared of you."

"Intrigued is more like it then." He puckered up at me. I was about to mush his face away, until he grabbed me by the wrist. The grip he had on it spoke volumes. It wasn't tight, like hurting me, yet it was uncomfortable. It was like he was giving me fair warning. He wasn't one to be played with. I had news for him. I wasn't either.

"Tuh. Back up, Lah." I pushed against him.

"Stop calling me that shit." He gritted his teeth, his grip on my wrist getting tighter.

"Nigga, you were begging me not to say your legal name like I was the feds or something. Now, I can't call you Lah? What do you suppose I call you then?"

"I'd love for you to call me daddy. We're not there yet so for now, call me boss."

"And if I don't call you, boss?" I raised my eyebrows with a challenging look.

"You'll just have to wait and see, huh?" He smirked. He stood there for a few minutes more. I knew if he didn't move, I'd wet up Isi and Yanna's sink.

"Whatever. Move." I jumped down. Turning toward the sink, I shut the water off. Before I could turn back around, Lah had his dick pressed against my back and lips against my ear.

"You gon' learn about me, ma."

His words sent chills down my spine. I wouldn't show him he had me a little spooked, though.

CHAPTER 15
KEN-YONA

It was going on three weeks now, and I still hadn't heard from Rell. At first, I wasn't worried. Whenever he called himself mad at me, he ran away to his family's house. Ugh, I wish this nigga would just grow up. Like, news flash! Your family ain't always going to be there!

Was I running to my mama every time we had a problem? No! It wasn't fair that he had his family to run to and I didn't. It was cool, though. I had a plan for him and his family. Yep, the Casique's were going to feel me. They were going to wish they were never mean to a bitch like me. All I needed was for this nigga to marry me already. The sooner he did, the better. Since he wasn't moving fast enough for me, I had to get shit popping on my own.

Pulling the pregnancy test I'd gotten from Dollar Tree out the box, I smiled at it. In front of me, there was a half glass full of warm tap water. Next to the glass, I had two different types of hot sauce. One was Tabasco, and the other was Tapatio.

After dumping a little of both hot sauces inside the

water, I held the pregnancy test inside the water for a few seconds. Once I took it out, I smiled at the test. This shit was easier than I thought it would be. Lowkey, I felt like a real-life scientist, mixing up experiments in my kitchen.

Holding the test at an angle, I snapped a picture of it. Before sending it to Rell, I did a little photo tweaking. Once it was to my liking, I sent it to Rell in a test that read: *Baby, I'm freaking out! I need you now. I don't know what to do...*

I didn't hold my breath for him to text back right away. It was noon, so I knew he was at work right now.

"Hello," I cooed into the receiver once he picked up.

"What's up, ma?"

"I want you...now."

"Slide through, baby."

"Here I come."

Before I left, I made sure to clean my little mess up. I didn't want to risk Rell coming home and seeing it. If he did, my ass was good as dead. He wouldn't physically hurt me. Just financially. My ass would be in the streets so fast with no pot to piss in or a window to throw it out of.

My side nigga was no use. He didn't have money except what he nickel and dimed for. Rell's money was long. It was able to take care of me for a lifetime. The house we lived in was five bedrooms and four and a half bathrooms. I told Rell I wanted something bigger, but he settled for this shit. Anyway, it was cute for what it was worth. There was a pool that went up to six feet deep, and a basement that was split between a full gym, laundry room, and theater room.

Rell had a room specifically for his 'niggas', i.e. his brothers. That was one thing about him I kind of liked, though. He didn't hang with outside niggas. It was just family with him. That was also what I hated most. He hung with his brothers and his she-man little sister so much, he could give two fucks about me.

As I said, it was cool. I'd continue to play my role—second to the Casique's. It was going to be funny when their shit came crashing down. They wouldn't know what hit them.

CHAPTER 16
RELL

I was sitting at my desk trying to focus on the paperwork in front of me. It was hard because my thoughts were all jacked up. It was the middle of the week, and this shit should've been looked over and sent to Pops a couple days ago. Surprisingly, he wasn't riding me about it. In fact, he wasn't riding any of us too much lately. After coming back from vacation, he seemed chill. From what Liz told us, he knew everything that was going on.

Other than getting this work done, Rizz had been heavily on my mind. The fact that she wasn't speaking to me pissed me off the fullest. We could be in the same room and she wouldn't say a word to me. I kept it cool around everyone and still nodded at her. See, this was the petty shit women did after a few nights of sex.

Honestly, I didn't know what she was so mad about. Her question kept playing in my head. I'd told her I didn't know because it was too soon to tell. I mean, we'd just had sex. My mind was all over the place. I was trying to sort my feelings out. I was stuck between how good it felt being with her and how bad I felt that I betrayed Keyona.

Keyona was a different story, man. I didn't know where we stood, or if we stood at all. After the night I left her ass in the house and went to Isi's, I'd been avoiding talking to her. She didn't seem too pressed to speak to me either, though. I hadn't heard from her ass in a good week. That alone made me wonder what the hell she'd been doing besides spending up money on this damn wedding.

See, that was another thing. I'd told her ass the wedding was off, and she was steady buying shit for it. I know because I paid close attention to my bank account. Every day, my funds were decreasing, all because she was buying some unnecessary shit.

Placing my hands over my face, I rubbed my eyes. I then opened my desk drawer and pulled my phone out. I had two text messages waiting on me. One was from Pops, and the other was Keyona. I opened Pops' first because I was anxious to see what he wanted. I was praying he wasn't going to say anything about the paperwork I was supposed to had been done.

Pops: *Come to Selma's @7:30 for dinner. Don't be late and don't bring your bitch.*

I laughed a little at the last part. Pops was always straightforward with us. That could be a blessing and a curse, all in one. Either way, his word was law. I was going to be at dinner, Keyona-free. Next, I checked Keyona's text. A part of me didn't want to look. I wasn't ready to deal with her yet. The other part of me, the side that loved the fuck out of her, wouldn't allow me to ignore her text.

Keyona: *Baby I'm freaking out! I need you now. I don't know what to do...*

Attached was a picture of a positive pregnancy test. At that moment, my whole world stopped. Dropping my phone on the desk, I was in pure shock. I wasn't mad at all. Surprised was more like it. I didn't know how to feel about this. I knew the baby was mine. That wasn't the issue I was having, though.

Keyona was on the IUD. She'd been on it since we got together. This whole time we'd been together, she'd never — not once — ended up pregnant. Again, I wasn't mad, just surprised. I was waiting for the happiness to kick in. It wasn't coming. This shit had to be a sign.

"Y'all are awfully quiet. Care to share some thoughts?" Pops asked myself, Isi, and Lah as we all nursed the drinks in front of us. My mind was stuck on that pregnancy test. I couldn't believe it. I was going to be a daddy.

Lah broke our silence and shrugged. "There's not much to talk about."

To me, he was a bit off. If anybody was going to be talking shit tonight, I knew it was going to be his shit-talking ass. Tonight, though, he was quiet. Just to take my mind off my own problems, I got in his business.

"What's wrong with you?"

He shook his head. "Nothing. I'm just vibin, is all."

"Bullshit. That nigga mad because Kori ain't fucking with his ass," Isi blurted, blasting him out the water. Lah flipped Isi the bird.

"You a fucking lie. I ain't even thinking about that girl."

"This nigga!" Isi and I laughed together. Lah, with his

cry baby ass, was in his feelings. He was mimicking our laughs and waving us off.

Man, I'd never thought I'd see the day this man fell in love. I wouldn't say it out loud because he'd deny the shit. He was in love, though. Just looking at him, he was in his feelings over this girl. I bet he ain't even got the cookies yet.

"Did you even get the cookies yet?" Isi asked my thoughts out loud.

Lah looked at him with his lips pressed to the side. It was like one of those *don't ask stupid questions* looks. Isi put his hands up in defense.

"So, that explains why you've been acting like that. You got the cookies, and now she's treating you like a regular nigga." Pops hit the nail on the head.

"Man, whatever." Lah waved him off. Pops cracked up.

"Don't be like that, son. I know how you feel. It was the same way with your mother. She let me hit, then tried to split."

"So, what you do after that?" Lah asked, shifting in his seat and leaning forward. He was staring Pops right in the mouth. Shit was funny because he swore he wasn't worried about Kori. Lying ass.

"What you mean, what I do? I handled mine. I told her ass once she let me hit, it was a done deal. She tried to play me like a bitch nigga, but I showed her ass. She ain't crossed me since."

"So, how'd you show her who's boss?" Lah was still interested.

"Isi," Pop said.

Isi answered, "Huh?"

"Nah, I'm saying you were how I got your mama to know I wasn't playing with her ass."

Me and Isi started laughing. Lah was sitting there looking ugly. He had this disgusted look on his face. "Ugh, I ain't getting Kori pregnant! I'm not ready for kids yet."

Again, we were laughing again.

"I thought you said you weren't thinking about her, little nigga," I called him out.

Lah side eyed me. "I'm not. I was just saying."

"He's lying!" Isi doubled over in hysterics.

"Whatever, man. Fuck y'all." Lah was back to being in his feelings. "So, how was the vacation, old man?"

"Oh, shit. Let me be the first to tell you. That way y'all don't hurt your mother's feelings when she announces it…" he stalled, looking around the table at each of us.

"Spit it out, nigga!" Lah anxiously blurted.

"Who the fuck you talking to?" Pops raised his voice. Lah got quiet. "Huh?"

"Nobody…" he lowly stated.

"Thought so. Anyway, your mama wants to have another baby." Pops revealed.

"What?!" we exclaimed in unison. Boom, there was another surprise. First, I find out about Keyona being pregnant. Now, my ma wants to have another baby. Wasn't she too old for all that shit?

"No offense, Pops. Aren't you and Ma too old to be popping out more kids?" I voiced my own thoughts.

"Yeah, ain't y'all niggas like fifty and shit?" Lah was right behind me with the questions. Isi was sitting there, staring off into space. I couldn't read his expression. It was between surprised and confused.

"I'm fifty, yes. She's only forty-two."

"She can still have babies and shit?" Lah asked. It was like he was against it, but interested at the same time.

"Yeah, she can still have babies and shit," Isi finally spoke. Pops was about to say something, but Isi cut him off. "What made you want to have another baby, Pops?"

Pops damn near choked on the drink he was sipping on. "Nigga, did you not hear me say, your mama wanted another baby?"

"You know what. You're right." Isi nodded his head. "So, what made Ma want to have another baby?"

"We were walking on the beach and she seen this couple hugged up. The woman was pregnant while the guy was rubbing her belly. The next thing I know, she got my ass in the villa fucking me better than a porn star."

Before I could swallow my drink, I spit it back into my cup. "Pops, too much information!"

"Oh, shut up! The way you and Rizz were going at it in my office, I know your ass knows a thing or two about a few positions. Made a whole fucking porno on my desk!"

"Whooaaa, whaaatt?!" Isi and Lah instigated. These niggas already knew what had went down.

I told them the night we all stayed over Isi and Yanna's crib. The girls were gone and they wanted to know what was wrong with me. They wouldn't leave me alone until I told them. I had explained what went down the night of Pops' birthday party. I broke everything down, from the next night to the next week, so they knew. They also knew that Rizz wasn't fucking with me. Since the day I kicked her out my car, she hadn't said much to me. If it wasn't work related, it didn't matter to her.

"Shut up y'all asses up! Pops, how you know that shit?"

"I keep cameras all over the building. My office isn't discriminatory." He shook his head with a smirk. "Can I ask you something, though, son?"

I looked him in the eyes and waited. "Anything."

"Why you with Keyona? I mean, a dead man can see your heart is with Rizz. It always has been. You're just the only one who refuses to see it."

I shook my head in a rapid motion. "Nah, it's not even like that with us. We had one or two sexual encounters. That's it, I'm telling y'all there are no feelings—"

"There she go right there with another nigga!" Lah pointed behind me. Quickly, I turned in my seat.

"Where?!" I damn near fell out my seat.

"Nigga, you whipped!" Isi and Lah shouted in unison.

"Fuck y'all! Ain't nobody whi—"

"Aye, sis. What's good?" Isi greeted Rizz as she approached the table. There was also some dude standing there with her. He had his arm on the small of her back. I watched his hands. His fingertips were two inches away from being on her ass.

"Hey y'all. Hey, Pops!" She hugged him only. I was watching her while Isi and Lah were watching me.

"Who is your friend?" Isi ended up asking her. I'm glad he did and not me. I couldn't believe her, man. She was out with whole nigga and never, not once, brought him by the mansion. If she was trying to be secretive to spare my feelings, it was only making it worse. My feelings…did I have feelings for her? This was something I was still trying to figure out.

Shaking my head, I focused back on the conversation. The entire time, my eyes were fixated on Rizz's. She was trying her hardest to avoid my eyes.

"Oh, I'm sorry. This is—"

"Her man, Sean." ol' dude cut her off and made his own introduction. The look on Rizz's face was priceless. It was like, *nigga when?*

Growing up with Rizz, I knew my best friend like the back of my hand. You couldn't tell me shit because I already knew it. Right now, she was irritated. She probably hadn't put a label on their relationship. This nigga would be lucky if she didn't walk out this restaurant right now.

Clearing her throat, she formed a smile. "Yeah, this my man, Sean. Sean, this is my Pops. These are my brother's Isi and Lah, and this is *their* brother, Israel."

Their? Did this bitch—if looks could kill, her and her *man* would be corpses on this fucking floor.

"What's good?" he held his hand out to me first. I stared at it with a grimace. Ain't fucking shaking this nigga hand. Fuck out of here. He noticed I wasn't going to be friendly and moved on to Lah.

Just like I knew, baby bro wasn't feeling him either. Sean was about to just say fuck it and take his hand back, until Isi caught it.

"What's up, my dude. Nice to meet you." His ol' friendly ass.

"Same here, man."

"Anyway, it was good seeing y'all." She tried to brush off. Pops called her name before she got away. He didn't speak until she turned around.

"I need to see you. Come by the mansion when you're free."

"Okay, Pops. I got you. I'll be there for teatime with Mama anyway." She gave him another hug.

Don't ask me what *teatime with Mama* was. I wanted to

know what Pops wanted to talk to Rizz about. She was his investment banker, yes. However, it seemed like he wanted to talk about more. Pulling my phone out, I hit Liz up.

Me: *I need you to do something for me.*

Liz: *What's up bro?*

Me: *Look into Rizz's new nigga. Any update on the nigga inquiring?*

Liz: *I met her dude. I'm not a fan. I'll look him up. No update, I swear I'm working on it!*

Me: *Aight sis. I love you and thanks.*

Liz: *No doubt. I love you too!*

We sat around the table a little while longer. Pops mainly wanted to discuss business-related shit. Occasionally, we'd joke on him about something random. Other than that, it was all black and white.

He never brought up the people inquiring about us. I knew he knew, though. I was curious as to why he hadn't discussed it with us. Maybe he trusted us to take care of the situation.

CHAPTER 17
LAH

Pops, Isi, and Rell had me fucked up. I wasn't tripping over no bitch. Kori might've been fine as fuck and cool people. I wasn't jumping over a bridge for her ass, though.

"Lah, pay attention to me. I didn't come all the way over here for you to ignore me," the female I had over whined.

"I'm focused. You just focus on sucking my dick," I spat.

"Mmkay daddy," she replied, and then swallowed my dick whole.

We were five minutes into her sucking me up, and I wasn't feeling it anymore. The crazy part about it was, my dick was reacting but my mind wasn't all there. It was in one place. If I say it, y'all going to try and call me a sucka.

"Aye, aye, back up, Kas. I'm not feeling this shit anymore." I pushed her head away and slipped my dick back into my pants.

Kas stood up with her hands on his thick hips. Even

with her standing here in front of me butt ass naked, I wasn't moved. There was a time I'd have her ass riding my pole with my finger in her booty hole. This bitch was bad. She was built like Blac Chyna, but her shit was natural. She didn't have silicone oozing out her ass or titties. Though her body was built, she was average in the face. I'm not gon' say she not cute or nothing, because she is. Her body is what got me, though.

"The fuck do you mean you ain't feeling it? You had me come way out to your house for nothing. You know I don't like my time being wasted, Lah!"

Standing up, I towered her 5'6 frame. "You better stop yelling in my shit too! Look, I said I ain't feeling it right now. I'll send you home in an Uber and slide you a stack."

"What? I look like some cheap hoe to you, Lah?"

I stared her up and down. She hadn't tried to put her trench coat back on. "I mean, you came over to my crib naked, shorty."

Slap!

"Fuck you! Don't act like you—"

I had her ass by the throat within milliseconds. There were only two women that I would ever let hoe me the way she just did. My mother and grandma, who was Mama to all of us. Imagine the way I was feeling since this bitch decided to put her little hands in my face. I'm a light-skinned nigga. I knew that shit was going to leave a bruise. When it did, Kas had better be hiding good. I didn't need to hit women. That's what I had sisters and a mother for.

With my hands still around her throat, I backed her ass up until we reached the elevator. I pressed the button and the doors slid open. Pushing her inside, I released her.

"Lah! Wait baby! I'm sorry!" She began to plead like a little bitch. I held no sympathy, nor emotion for her. She knew she'd fucked up. I was about to press the button for her to head down. She tried to come out, but I pushed her back in. Quickly, I pressed the button with her screaming.

"Wait! I'm naked! I need my coat, Lah—"

"Yes, hello Mr. Casique..." the sexy ass receptionist answered in a smooth tone.

"Um, yes, I just wanted to give you a heads up. There's a naked and deranged woman headed down in the elevators. She just tried to break into my house. You might want to call the police or some type of security. She's going to be acting a damn fool and try to come back up here."

"Okay, sir. Thanks for the heads up. I have Chicago PD on speed dial."

Smiling into the receiver, I replied. "No problem, ma. I'm just doing my civic duty."

After hanging up, I hit Liz up. Since it was a Friday night, I knew she was getting into something. I was also calling to get some information about *you know who.*

"What's up, big head boy?" she cheerfully greeted into the phone. I could hear people all around on the other end.

"What you doing, little head?"

"Nothing. We having girl's night at Rizz's." She giggled. "Shanah, stooop!"

"Since when you start kicking it with her again?" My nose flared, thinking about the situation at the club from weeks ago. This was the first time I'd heard her mention anything about her. We hadn't heard anything about her cousin or whatever since everything went down.

"Who said we ever stopped kicking it?" she asked with amusement in her tone.

"I just thought because you haven't mentioned her name."

"Oh nah, we still good. *Thinking leaves you stinking,*" she quoted Pops at the end. I nodded. She was right. I walked right into that one.

"What about her people?" I skeptically inquired. I was now standing in front of the sink with the water on. I was running water into my hand and dumping it into the sink.

"What about her? Shanah said she don't even be kicking it with her like that. That night at the club was the first time in forever. Of course, she stayed behind because Shane is family. That's about it, though."

"That's cool and all, but what's ol girl up to?" I was referring to Shane.

"She gon' keep her mouth closed and stay out the way, bet that," Liz said in a serious tone.

I already knew what she was getting at. "How much?"

"Ten thousand," she simply said. I assumed it would've been more. Again, as Pops said, *thinking leaves you stinking.* In other words, never assume, always know.

"Well damn. Who all over there?" I changed the subject.

"Me, Shanah, Rizzy, and Yanna," she gladly answered.

I was happy to hear Yanna was in the mix. It was good that sis got out. I wasn't sure how she was truly feeling since the miscarriage. She kept a smile on her face. Who knew how she was really feeling, though? Isi seemed cool, for the most part. Then again, he was the oldest. He specialized in keeping a brave face on. Pops always said if something happened to him, look to Isi. Sometimes, I was happy I was one of the youngest. Being the oldest seemed like a lot of work.

"Oh, that's it, huh?" I was a little disappointed to not hear *you know who's* name. I hadn't heard or seen her since the sleepover. That was damn near two weeks ago. I hoped her new job was working out for her.

"Yep."

"So, that's all?"

"Yeah, nigga. That's what I said."

Don't get smart in the mouth, muthafucka," I half joked.

cough "Kori is at home." *cough, cough*

This nigga here. I shook my head laughing. "What made you tell me that?"

"I don't know what you mean. I have to go, bro. Hit me up tomorrow." She hung up.

Now, I was standing here thinking about my next move. I wanted to go to Kori's. Then again, I didn't know what I'd say when I got there. I never had this problem before. I did and said whatever I wanted. What made her so different? *Fuck it*, I thought. I'm just gon' wing it.

CHAPTER 18
KORI

Here it was, going on midnight and I was working on some shit that wasn't in my job description. Originally, I was happy to be working with my newest client. She's cool, upbeat, and the pay is good. What's not to love? That is, until she started giving me other tasks. At first, I was down to help. I'm like, why not? Now, I just felt like a secretary. She had me running to get her coffee, reading over various amounts of paperwork, and now here I was, setting up and promoting her new business page on Facebook. *People can only do what you allow*, my mother's infamous words played in my head. She was right. I allowed Kassidy to treat me like this.

I remember, just a couple weeks ago, I was happy to be working with her. Now, I wish I never accepted her proposal. Besides the pay being great, this job sucked!

"Oh shit, this nigga can sing?!" I jumped off my bed and got closer to the TV.

I'd spent the day catching up on the current season of Empire. I was just now on the last episode where Cookie and Luscious got back together. Now, he was singing to her on the stage. I got all mushy on the inside. I loved to see love. It always made me think of what it'd be like to have someone love me the way I deserved. I'd had boyfriends. They were nothing to brag about, though. That was way back when I was in my high school days. I hadn't entertained anyone since being in Chicago. Well, Lah, but I wouldn't call that nothing but crazy.

I was sitting on the toilet, getting ready to wipe when I heard a loud thud come from downstairs. I lived out in Lincoln Park, in brick row houses. It had an upstairs and downstairs. When I walked out my front door, there was a big park across the street. It had big trees and lots of room to play or have a picnic.

Flushing the toilet, I assumed it was one of the neighbors. They all had kids, so it wasn't uncommon for me to hear a little banging here and there. Walking out of the bathroom, I heard it again. This time, I was sure it came from my house.

I know I locked the door, I thought to myself as I crept down the stairs. I got to the bottom stair and grabbed this sculpture made of stone off the banister. As I neared the kitchen, I could see a small light shining. It wasn't that bright. I knew it had to be the fridge or stove light.

"Who's there?" I shouted, getting closer.

Nobody said anything. I heard a lot of rummaging around, though. I was convinced there was a beast of some sort in my kitchen. Then again, how did they get the stove light on? I always turned it off before going to bed. How did they get the fridge door open?

"Hello!" I poked my head around the corner in the entrance of the kitchen.

I had wooden floors that sometimes creaked when you walked on them. With all the walking I was doing, whoever was in my house should've been running for cover by now.

I could see someone bent over, digging in the fridge drawers. "What the hell?!"

Just as I was raising the sculpture over my head to slam it into the person's back, they stood all the way up. I now knew it was a man. He turned around, and I was glaring into the eyes of Lah. I was infuriated! One, he'd broken into my home. Two, he didn't respond and say it was him. I could've killed his stupid ass!

"Islah, I swear you better have a good reason for being in my damn kitchen," I huffed, slamming the sculpture down.

"Ma, you was going to hit me with that shit?" he smirked, completely disregarding what I said. That pissed me off more than him breaking in. How was he going to break in and then play like everything was cool? Ugh, I swear I was so over this dude.

"Hell yes I was going to hit your ass! Now, tell me what you're doing here. Why you break into my house!?"

I noticed he had a whole sandwich in his hand. It had lettuce, tomato, cheese, bacon, mayo, and smoked turkey on it. "Stop eyeballing my sandwich, ma. If you want one, I'll make you one."

"No, what I want is to know why you broke into my house? I could call the cops you know!"

"Ahh, you could. But you won't. I could've very well done the same thing, ma. I didn't, though." he shrugged, nonchalant in his tone. Nothing irked me more than that. I was pissed and he wasn't taking me seriously. This inconsiderate bastard!

"Whatever! Why are you here, Lah?"

"Who here? My name Islah. I don't know any Lah's. That your new nigga or something?" he grinned, chewing on the sandwich. It was more than halfway gone now. Damn, he had to hungry to be inhaling food like that.

I rolled my eyes, knowing what he was getting at. This was the second situation where he'd told me to call him Islah and not Lah. See, this was one of the reasons I couldn't fuck with him like that. He was ass backwards. The first time I called him Islah, he jumped down my throat, telling me to call him Lah. Now, he didn't want me calling him that.

"I'm sick of you. You're the most irritating person I've met! You say and do shit that makes no sense. You think you own the world and everything in it. It's fucking annoying and—"

He shut me up by putting his lips on top of mine. For a moment, I allowed his plush pillow-like lips to hump mine. I even let his tongue explore inside my mouth some. Letting a moan escape, I came to.

Slap!

"No! You don't get to do that!" I pushed him away.

He came back, this time closer. He had his body pressed against mine. I hated that my lady parts always reacted to him. The smell of his Jimmy Choo cologne made me sick with pleasure. Who wears cologne this time of night anyway? His uglass, that's who!

Then, his stupid dark brown eyes had to be so sexy. Standing under his gaze made me uncomfortable. I hated that shit. I could usually stand with the best of them. With him, I would always become nervous and have to get away.

"Move, Lah..." There I went, moaning again. He didn't move. He stood there, staring at me. The fact that I couldn't read him irritated me more.

"Lah, move!" I pushed him back. He grabbed me by the wrist.

"Watch it, ma. The last female who put her hand on me is in jail now." With the way he said it, I knew he wasn't lying. Releasing my wrists, he buried his face in my neck. He inhaled my scent. I stared into space with a bored expression.

Yanna and Liz's words replayed in my mind. I swear this shit wasn't fair. I didn't ask for a crazy nigga to stalk my life. I know I didn't help the situation by breaking into his house, but still. This was some bullshit. The messed-up part was, I don't even know how all this started.

"Lah—Islah," I quickly corrected myself. "Please move."

"You don't want me to move. If you did, I wouldn't be standing here." He picked me up and placed me on the sink. Like the hoes they wanted to be for him, my legs opened, and he gladly stood between them. "See, look. You want this shit."

"No, you want—"

"Shh." He stood there with his head still buried in my neck. The next thing I heard was water running. *Oh hell no!* I began to panic and squirm in his grasp because I didn't know his motives. He might've been trying to drown me.

"What are you doing? Get off me!" I fought against him. He was too strong.

"Aye, calm that shit down! I turned the water on

because it helps me keep calm. What did you think? I was going to drown your little ass?"

"Hell yes, nigga!" I honestly blurted.

He began to laugh out loud. He still had me in his grasp. I swear his dick was laughing too. I felt it moving against my womanhood and became turned on.

"You're wild, ma. How I'm going to drown your ass in this sink? You too big." He was laughing harder now.

"I don't know. You might've tried to flip me and place my head under the water or something. There's plenty of ways to drown someone."

"Well, that's not it, mama. I had to gather my thoughts right quick."

"That's crazy because I run water to clear my mind too."

"Real shit?" he asked like he didn't believe me.

"Mhm." I nodded. "Why you had to gather your thoughts?"

"I um…" His voice trailed off. "I don't know how to say this shit."

Hearing the pressure of the water die down some, I turned to see why. He was letting it run in his hand and dumping it back into the sink.

I grabbed his hand. It was clear that he was nervous and didn't know how to say what he wanted to say. I went to turn to the water off and he snatched my hand away.

"Leave it."

"Tell me what's on your mind," I demanded, staring into his eyes.

"I like you…" he inaudibly revealed. I heard him but wanted to hear it again.

"What?" I was shocked. You damn right I wanted to hear it again.

"You heard me, ma. Not going to repeat the shit."

Rude ass! I screamed in my head. "I don't know what to say, Islah."

"Don't say nothing. I just wanted to put it out there." He then turned the water off. "Please don't say it back unless you mean in. I hate when people say shit because they feel obligated."

"I got you." I smiled at him. "I just wouldn't have guessed you liked me like that."

"Don't ruin the moment by being corny either. I'll take my like back." He stared me in the eyes. Just by the look in his eyes, I knew he wasn't playing with me.

"I'm just saying. You're so rude to me. Then, you play with my emotions like all the time. I've never met anyone who shows their *like* the way you do."

"You're right. You also haven't met a nigga like me. Probably never will," he cockily announced.

"You're right. The other niggas got more sense." I laughed.

He laughed too. "Yeah, them the boring ones."

"Whatever. You're just crazy."

"You call it crazy. I call it me." He shrugged. I looked away with a half-smile. "Look ma, I don't know how this relationship shit works. I've never been somebody's *boyfriend* or whatever. I just know I like you. I'm going to act however I see fit. I hope you're ready. I told you that I like you. That means pretty much anything that goes in a relationship."

I stared at this man, waiting for him to break character and smile. He didn't. That told me enough. "So, basically, you're telling me that we're *not* in a relationship, but I need to act like it because you *like* me?"

"Aww, very good baby. You got it! Gold star for you!" he sarcastically exclaimed.

"Umm, no. I don't got it. Neither do you. If you got me acting like I'm in a relationship, *we're in a relationship*. You're not about to be out here fucking on bitches and I can't do the same!"

"First, lower your voice when talking to me. All that yelling shit won't fly this way. You gon' learn today. Second, who said I was gon' be fucking on anything? You didn't even give me a chance. Like I said, I don't know nothing about relationships. I'd like to learn, though. I'm not going to get it right all the time, but you can teach a nigga. So, let's go slow, aight?"

I nodded my head and smiled. "Aight."

"Now, come suck my dick." He smirked.

"Get the fuck out of here!" I burst into laughter.

For the rest of the night, we went back and forth, throwing playful insults. We stayed up until three in the morning, talking about any and everything that came to mind. I learned a little bit about him. Lah wasn't as bad as he made himself out to be.

The next morning, I woke up in Lah's arms. We were on the couch with the TV going on low. I remember making him turn it on before we laid down. He wanted to sleep with it off. He said he liked the way the dark sounded. Whatever that means. I couldn't sleep without the TV or music playing in the background. It'd been like this since I was a kid. Islah was going to have to get used to it.

Peeking at the clock, I noticed it was only seven in the morning. I was going back to sleep when the house rang. Closing my eyes, I knew it could only be two people. It was either my mom or Kassidy Kyle- *my boss.*

I laid there for however long, thinking if I wanted to answer. I knew if I didn't, it could be my mom and she'd be worried if I didn't answer. I didn't care to answer Kassidy. I was thinking about quitting her. She treated me more like a secretary than anything. I mainly stayed because of the pay.

"Bae, answer the phone before I break it. Who even keeps a house phone? Nobody but your ass," Lah mumbled in his sleep.

I thought twice about slapping him, even playfully. He told me he'd slap my ass back if I kept slapping him. That was hours before we fell asleep, though. Still, I believed his ass.

"Whatever, Lah. Shut up!"

I was getting up to get the phone until Islah grabbed me and pinned me on the couch.

"Who?" He stared me deep in the eyes. Our faces were so close I could smell his morning breath.

"Your breath stinks. I got an extra toothbrush you can use in the bathroom." I giggled. Being an asshole, he blew his breath in my face.

"Eww, nasty! Get off me!"

"Mhm, answer your punk ass landline, nigga."

"Whatever *nigga*," I mimicked under my breath. He came back and got in my face.

"What?"

He had me pinned down on the couch, laying on top of me now. "Nothing, move! Go brush your teeth, stinky."

Before moving, he stole a kiss. I couldn't help the smile or happiness that stole my mood. Lah was irritating as hell. I couldn't deny the way he made me feel though. The shit was crazy. Just a few weeks ago, I swore I wanted nothing to do with him. Now I was allowing him to break into my house, eat up my food and kiss me with stank breath. I know the shit sounds crazy and probably stupid as hell. I know, but I don't care. I want to see where this could go.

I still didn't know whether we were in a relationship or not. The way he explained it was weird. That was Lah though. Crazy ass.

"Hello," finally I answered my 'landline', as Lah said.

"Kori!" It was Kassidy.

"Yes, Ms. Kyle?" I tried to keep a professional tone with her. Lord knew, I wanted to hang up in this bitch face. I mean, look how she was already screaming on me. Bitch, you called me! Not the other way around.

"I need you to come get me. I'm at the precinct. I have no money or clothes. For some reason, I remembered your number by heart."

Yeah bitch, because you always ringing my damn phone, I thought with a roll to my eyes.

"Jail? How'd you end up there?" I decided I was going to toy around with this heffa right quick.

"My boyfriend locked me out the house last night because—" She stopped herself from talking. *"That's none of your business!* Just come and get me!" She hung up. I looked at the phone like it was the one who yelled at me and expected me to come pick it up.

I swear this bitch was a pill. I had a right mind to leave her in jail. Instead, the good in me wouldn't allow me to do that. I was taught that good karma comes to those who give it. I wasn't going to let Kassidy Kyle or anybody mess that up for me.

Islah had come out the bathroom. He stood in front of me. His cologne was lingering around, playing with my senses. He was wearing the white wife beater he wore under his clothes with some plaid blue and white boxers. This nigga even fell asleep with his chain on. *Lord, why he have to be so bomb with his uglass?*

"Who was that, and why you looking at the phone like that?"

I couldn't help but roll my eyes. Lah hated it. While we were talking last night, he told me it was a turn off. He claimed it took away from my 'sexiness'. "My bitch of a boss. She's in jail and wants me to bail her out."

"Damn." He took a seat next to me. "What I tell you about that eye rolling shit?"

I stared at him threw squinted eyes. Now wasn't the time for him to be trying to be bossy. "Anyways...I swear I can't stand her. I want to quit. I can't just yet because it wouldn't look good on my resume, and plus it's not like I have clients lined up outside my door." I let my head fall into my palms. I wanted to cry, kick, scream- just be dramatic to show my annoyance.

"Had you come to work like I told you to, you wouldn't be going through all of this." He shook his head.

"Boy, bye. You had me hauled out for being five minutes late!" I exclaimed, reminding him.

"Lower your voice," he warned in an even tone. No matter how loud I got with him, he never got loud back.

He stayed calm and cool. I found it low-key creepy. Then again, what didn't I find weird or creepy about this man? "I also told you to come back."

"Yeah, after the fact you thought you were going to get cussed out by dear old daddy." His face dropped when I said that. "Yeah, I heard you talking to your brothers and sister."

"I still offered you the job. Anyway, that's old shit. What you about to do about this?" he pointed at the phone, referring to Kassidy.

"I'm going to go bail this bitch out so I can keep my job. She paying me five grand a day." I was standing up to stretch.

He pulled me back down and onto his lap. "Wrong. You're going to leave that bitch in jail and come work with me. I can quadruple that shit."

"It's not that simple, Islah." I shook my head with doubt in my voice.

I wish it was that simple. The way Kassidy Kyle was set-up, she was bound to tarnish my name. My career would be over before it even started. Then who would hire me? He was offering me a job now, yeah. Who's to say he wouldn't have my ass hauled off again?

He kissed my lips a few times. "It is that simple. She don't run you. Plus, it's not like you have to deal with that. Trust me, leave the bitch in jail. Let her find her own way out."

"Well, what if she keeps calling? What if she tries to drag my name through the mud?" I asked out loud, voicing my fears.

"Fuck that bitch. I'll have her touched if she pulls anything like that." I knew he wasn't lying with the way he was staring into my eyes. They turned dark and cold. "As for the calling, it ain't shit to get a new number. I already told you about that house phone shit, anyways."

"My mama calls on it." I slightly whispered with worry.

"Get ma a cell. It's the twentieth century, baby."

"We'll see if she goes for that. I'm going to Portland to get her for the Fourth. I'll talk to her about it."

"Okay, and it's *we* going to Portland." He corrected me.

"Umm, I didn't invite you, nigga." I side eyed him with my face scrunched up.

"I know. I invited myself. I can't have my girl out on another city trying to rekindle old flames and shit. Don't play with me, Kori." He looked at me dead in the face.

"So, I'm your girl now?" I was staring at him with a bored expression, trying to hide my true feelings. I can't lie. I liked the way it sounded falling out his mouth. All sexy and demand and shit.

"That's what I said, ain't it?" his tone, nor his facial expression changed.

"Boy, please." I smirked, trying to get up. He pulled me back down and kept me in a tight hold.

"I'm not playing, Kori."

"Okay, Islah. I heard you."

Silently, we had a stare down. He held the same facial expression. I smiled, trying to get him to smile. He didn't, so I left it alone. Lord, what did I get myself into in dealing with this man? Only time would tell.

"Why are we going to the doctors, Rell? You don't believe me when I say I'm pregnant? What would I have to lie for, huh?" Keyona nagged in the passenger seat.

Pulling up to stop light, I blew out a deep sigh. She'd been complaining about this shit since I came home last night. She had dinner prepared, which was unusual. Keyona could cook her ass off. She used to make me meals all the time. Since I was spending time with my family now, she stopped. I asked her why. Her reply was, *eat wherever you at* or *didn't you eat with your family?* I swear I was starting to think she was jealous of them, like she didn't have a place in my life or something. I loved Keyona. I tried to show her that shit all the time, but she would brush it off. I was starting to think she didn't really want to be with me anymore.

"I believe you, baby. I just want to go to the doctors. This way, they can see if everything is okay with the baby."

"Okay, so after the doctors, we going to the dress shop to pick up my new dress, right?"

"*New dress?!* Keyona, I swear we talked about this shit. You have enough dresses to choose from."

"No baby, I sent all the other ones back. I'm sure about this one."

"Alright ma, whatever you want. Let's just deal with one thing at a time." I nodded, paying her no mind. I was trying to agree to disagree with her. There was no need to stress her out. From what I knew, if the mother was stressed, it went to the baby as well. I didn't want my child stressed. It wasn't even developed yet.

"Okay baby, but I really don't want to go to the doctor today. Besides, I have my own doctor. I'll make an appointment in the morning, okay?" she pleaded in a whiny tone. I wasn't going for it. We were going to see this doctor, whether she wanted to or not.

"No, babe. We're already here. It'll be quick. They're going to give you some prenatal vitamins, and we're going to get to hear the baby's heartbeat." I was looking forward to hearing my baby's heartbeat. I was still taking in that I was about to be someone's daddy. To be honest, I thought Isi and Yanna would be the first to have a baby. Since the miscarriage, I didn't know anymore. They hadn't said much about having a baby. The other night at dinner, I wanted to ask Isi. I decided against it because I was almost positive it was a touchy subject. I mean, if it were me, I wouldn't want to dwell on it either. My biggest concern was Yanna. Like, how was she taking it overall? In front of the fam, she was legit. Who knew how she acted behind closed doors?

"Come on, baby. Why are you acting like this? You

barely pregnant and already acting bitchy. You hungry or something?" I looked to Keyona with raised eyebrows. She glared at me.

"Fuck you, Rell! I'll go into this stupid appointment since you insist." She opened the car door.

Just when I was about to open mine, my phone rang in the cup holder. I would've ignored it, but since we had time before the appointment started, I went ahead and answered.

"What's up, sis?" I hit the speaker button and answered. It was Liz.

"Bro, are you busy?" She asked with panic.

"Nah, I have an appointment with Keyona in a few. What's up?"

"I found some shit out."

"About Rizz's new nigga?" I anxiously inquired. Keyon hadn't gotten out of the car yet. She was listening and sucking her teeth.

"No, about the nigga who been inquiring about our name."

"Oh, who?" I was just as anxious about that shit. I did want to know more about this Sean nigga, though.

"His name is Tech. Well, that's what the streets call him anyway. He's been in town for a few months and has been trying to hit a lick." she explained.

"What?" I was shocked by the news.

"Right, I know. I'm doing some extra digging. I should have a location on this nigga soon." She informed me.

"Alright, sis."

"Hello! We have an appointment." Keyona waved her hand in my face, as if I couldn't see her sitting there rolling her eyes.

"Baby, we got fifteen minutes. Hold up and we'll go inside," I told Keyona, then went back to Liz. "Hey, sis. Keep going…"

"Yeah, so I was also able to find out that he hangs with a female. Now, I haven't quite figured out who she is. When I do, I'll hit you, Isi and Lah up."

"Right, then we can snatch that bitch and get her to—"
Bink!

Feeling something hard crash into the back of my head, I was in a daze. My vision was blurred, but I could still hear my sister calling out to me.

"Rell…Rell, you still there? Hello?"

To Be Continued…